The Emily Carr Mystery

Books by Eric Wilson

The Tom and Liz Austen Mysteries

Also available by Eric Wilson

The Emily Carr Mystery

A Liz Austen Mystery

by

ERIC WILSON

HarperCollins*Publishers*Ltd

As in his other mysteries, Eric Wilson writes here about imaginary people in a real landscape.

Find Eric Wilson at www.ericwilson.com

The Emily Carr Mystery
Text copyright © 2001 by Eric Hamilton Wilson.
Copyright renewed 2003 by Eric Wilson Enterprises, Inc. All rights reserved.

Published by HarperCollins Publishers Ltd

First published in trade paperback by HarperCollins Publishers Ltd 2001. This mass market paperback edition 2002.

HarperCollins books may be purchased for educational, business, or sales promotional use through our Special Markets department.

HarperCollins Publishers Ltd
2 Bloor Street East, 20th Floor
Toronto, Ontario, Canada
M4W 1A8

www.harpercanada.com

National Library of Canada Cataloguing in Publication

Wilson, Eric, 1940–
    The Emily Carr mystery / Eric Wilson.

ISBN 0-00-639190-7

            I. Title.

PS8595.I583E55 2002   jC813'.54   C2002-902417-X
PZ7

WEB 10 9 8 7 6 5 4 3 2

Printed and bound in Canada

cover design by Richard Bingham
cover and chapter illustrations © 2001 by Richard Row
logo photograph by Heath Moffat © 2003 eweInc.

For my dear wife, Flo,
and our friend Sadie

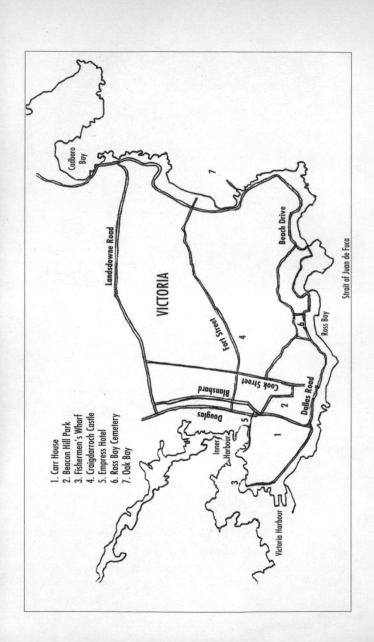

1. Carr House
2. Beacon Hill Park
3. Fishermen's Wharf
4. Craigdarroch Castle
5. Empress Hotel
6. Ross Bay Cemetery
7. Oak Bay

VICTORIA

Cadboro Bay

Landsdowne Road

Fort Street

Beach Drive

Blanshard

Cook Street

Douglas

Dallas Road

Inner Harbour

Victoria Harbour

Ross Bay

Strait of Juan de Fuca

1

Our boat was the greatest—a classic cruiser called the *Amor de Cosmos*.

But I wasn't happy.

I almost screamed as our cruiser heeled over. Cold spray whipped my face as we raced through the night. I grabbed for support, thinking I'd tumble into the dark sea waters.

From above, on the command bridge, came laughter. It was my friend Tiffany, who was feeling good. Tiff was beside the man she soon would marry—Paris de-Mornay. As I watched, Paris fed more horsepower to the twin turbocharged diesels—our cruiser leapt forward even faster through the waves, making me stagger.

Paris was movie-star handsome. A spotlight shone on his perfect face as he smiled at Tiffany. Paris was

22 and wore shorts, a sweater, and a gold necklace. Apparently his deck shoes had been shipped from an exclusive shop in Hawaii; Paris bought almost everything on the Internet.

The deMornay family was very wealthy, and so was Tiff's. The families were a unit, bonded together by the friendship of the two mothers. Paris was three years old when Tiffany was born; at the time the mothers quipped that eventually Paris and Tiffany should marry.

Then the family joke turned into reality. Tiff fell totally in love with Paris during her teens. It happened so easily—the families spent a lot of time together. Tiff and Paris made a natural couple.

Recently, though, tragedy had struck. Two years ago Paris lost his parents in a terrible car crash. He was especially devastated about his father, and Tiff had spent a lot of time consoling Paris. Then one day I learned that Tiffany had accepted his marriage proposal.

Now I was in Victoria for the wedding. But I was feeling upset—somehow, things didn't seem right. Sighing, I looked at the sky. A silvery moon watched from the glorious heavens; below, whitecaps raced across the waters.

"The lights of Victoria look so pretty from out here," I said to Tiffany, as she climbed down a ladder from the bridge. "Thanks for inviting me to British Columbia for your wedding. Imagine, two full weeks in Victoria—and I love it here."

Tiffany flashed her blue eyes my way. "That's wonderful, Liz." Tiny, blonde and pretty, 19 years old, she'd been raised in the exclusive world of the ultra-wealthy. With her own personal fortune Tiff could have bought and sold some countries, but she was the sweetest and most natural person. We'd met volunteering at a children's hospital in Winnipeg, and our friendship was the best. Tiff was two years older than me, but it didn't matter.

"Tiff," I said, "remember all those times Paris came to Winnipeg to see you? He was such a fun guy, and I was so happy about your wedding. But . . . somehow he's changed."

"Of course he has!" There was an edge to Tiff's voice, and I realized I'd touched a nerve. "How would you feel, Liz? His parents have died, and he's still grieving."

I braced myself against the rolling of the sea. "I guess you're right, Tiff. You know what? You always find the good in people."

"Liz, he needs me. Besides, I want children and a husband. I like the West Coast—I can be happy here." She lovingly touched her engagement ring. "Paris and I are in this together. Through the good times and the bad. We've got so much in common—"

Then Tiffany screamed. "*Look out*," she yelled at Paris. Tiff pointed across the sea. "That's the *Clipper*, and we're going straight at it!"

I stared at the *Clipper* as it raced out of the night. A high-speed catamaran carrying tourists between Seattle and Victoria, the *Clipper* rode above the water on two pontoons with an open space between.

Now I saw what Paris had planned—he was trying a daredevil stunt, aiming our boat directly at the space between the pontoons. "We'll never make it," I yelled into the shrieking wind. "Don't be crazy, Paris!"

Grinning, he fed more power to the diesels. From the *Clipper*, a loud horn split the night air—warning us of the danger. Tiffany and I grabbed the railing, horrified at the vision of the *Clipper* coming swiftly at us.

Suddenly our boat heeled over, changing course. With a laugh, and an arrogant wave of his hand at the other vessel, Paris took the *Amor de Cosmos* safely out of danger.

Grabbing the steel rungs of the ladder, I climbed to the command bridge. It rolled and pitched as Paris hotdogged the cruiser across the sea. Before him, on the control console, blue dials glowed.

"Listen, Paris," I said, "how about cutting back on the throttle."

"Sure, Liz, no problem."

The engines slowed, right down to a low growl. I heard whitecaps crashing against each other in the night.

"I was just having some fun," Paris added.

I didn't want to object once again to one of his stunts, so I said nothing about the *Clipper*. Instead, I commented, "This is a beautiful boat."

"It belonged to my father."

"You miss him, eh?"

"Yeah." Paris sighed.

"Listen," I said, "thanks for letting me stay at your estate while I'm in Victoria. That's generous of you, Paris."

"Hey, Liz, you're my fiancée's closest friend and one of her bridesmaids. I'm only sorry you can't be maid of honour. Why's that, anyway? Tiffany never told me."

"The maid of honour has to be at least 18 to sign the wedding register. I'm a year too young."

"I'm sorry about that," Paris said with genuine sympathy.

"Robbed of the chance to be maid of honour at my best friend's wedding. Gee, you could have waited a year! But Tiff wants wedding bells, and the pitter-patter of little feet."

Paris grinned. "Tiffany sure loves kids. Me, too. I want a son and heir. We'll name him for my father."

Then Paris opened his cell phone; it had commanded attention by loudly playing "Jingle Bells."

"Yes?" Paris said. He listened for a moment, then replied, "Four K on Bigoted Earl. That's all I can manage. Goodbye, now."

Turning to me, Paris smiled. "I was going to mention, Liz, a lot of smuggling happens here. I thought you'd be interested."

Paris looked across the water at the lights of a distant city, sparkling on the shoreline of the United States. Above, the Olympic Mountains rose into the night sky. White snow glowed on some peaks, even though it was summer.

"That's Port Angeles over there," Paris explained. "It's in the state of Washington." He turned toward Victoria. "I can always spot the smugglers—maybe we'll see one tonight. They come out of Canada, moving fast, with no running lights. They carry drugs, forged credit cards, illegal immigrants. If someone can make a buck smuggling, they'll do it. Personally, I think it's crazy."

Tiffany joined us on the command bridge. As she

cuddled against Paris, I took the other seat. From here, the view was beyond awesome. It was a total panorama—not a single tree or building blocked the horizon. I could see every star, even little faint ones. It was so romantic.

Tiffany snuggled closer to Paris. "Remember when you called me 'princess'? When we were kids? I loved that, Paris." She smiled at me. "We used to play wedding, and Paris would be the groom. I was Lady Diana."

Paris kissed her cheek. "Tiff, you'll always be my princess."

I smiled at him. "How'd you come up with your boat's name?"

"Amor de Cosmos was an actual dude, long ago. He arrived in British Columbia in the 19th century and ended up as premier, running the place. He started life as William Smith, then picked a new name—cool idea, eh? *Amor de cosmos* means 'lover of the universe.'"

Tiffany touched his dark hair. "That's a perfect description of you, sweetheart."

"My dad was quite the guy," Paris told me proudly. "A sports champion in his time, and adored by all the cuties. He bought this classic cruiser when he was young. The *Amor* has a cedar-strip hull on oak. I added the twin diesels for real power. They're turbocharged."

Tiffany glanced at her Rolex. "Let's head home, Paris. Daddy will be calling soon."

"Phone him on your cell, and we'll stay out longer."

Tiffany shook her head. "Daddy needs to know I'm safely home from the sea. Otherwise he won't be able to sleep."

"He's staying downtown at the Empress Hotel?" I asked.

Tiffany nodded. "Daddy loves that place."

Before long we approached Oak Bay, Victoria's luxurious neighbour. Through binoculars I studied the Oak Bay Beach Hotel, then the expensive mansions, houses, and condos along the shoreline. Lights glowed from the windows, looking cosy.

"What a sight under a full moon," Tiffany said. "It's like being in a dream."

"*Hey*," Paris exclaimed. Grabbing the binoculars from me, he looked north along the water in the direction of Thirteen Oaks, the estate owned by his family. "I see some boat, stopped abeam of my house. No running lights. Let's check this out."

"Could it be a smuggler?" I asked excitedly.

"Possibly."

"Be careful," Tiffany warned, as Paris fed maximum RPMs to the twin beasts that roared below decks. "This could be dangerous!"

We moved north along the shoreline, feeling the wind on our faces. As we approached the mystery craft, Paris studied it through his state-of-the-art night binoculars. "It's called the *Outlaw*. There's an open deck and a wheelhouse. Some guy's inside—I can see him. He's got blond hair and two gold earrings. Looks maybe 20 years old, 25 max."

Above the cliff stood an ancient mansion. Moonlight glowed on the ivy embracing its walls. The stone building was very large, dominating the enormous estate known as Thirteen Oaks. There were several chimneys; smoke curled from one. From the gardens of the estate, a crooked path led down to a beach. Nearby was a small island with no signs of habitation.

The *Amor de Cosmos* powered forward, moving in on the mysterious *Outlaw*. Suddenly a spotlight glared across the water. A man's voice yelled, "Clear away."

Paris swore angrily. Veins bulged in his throat as he screamed, "Forget it, jerk. And what exactly are you doing? I live in that house up there." The engines rumbled as Paris moved our craft closer. "Who are you, anyway?" he cried across the water. "Identify yourself."

Silence from the *Outlaw*. I gripped the railing, aware of the painful throbbing of my heart. I was so scared.

Then Tiffany screamed. "A gun! Paris, he's got a gun!"

I stared across the tossing waves. "Holy Hannah." A nickel-plated revolver shone in the spotlight's glow. "That thing looks real. Let's—"

Fire burst from the muzzle. Something hummed past into the night, and then I heard the shot. It was total confusion on our boat as I dove for cover beside Tiffany while Paris grabbed for the throttle, and our cruiser leapt away across the waves.

"That was a real bullet," I yelled.

Paris looked behind. "He's coming after us, but we'll outrun him. This baby can really move."

The other boat fell away into the night as we escaped north. Then, without warning, the mighty roar of our engines turned to a coughing gasp, followed by utter silence. Out in the night, we heard the *Outlaw* coming our way.

2

"We're out of fuel," Paris yelled. "We'll have to swim for it."

Paris hurried forward to drop the anchor. Kicking off his deck shoes, he glanced toward the nearby shoreline. Then he dove into the night. His body describing a perfect arc, Paris sliced down into the sea—then surfaced.

"You next, Tiffany," he cried from the waves. "I'll swim with you, but hurry. I can see the spotlight. He's coming fast!"

Moments later, Tiffany was in the water and swimming toward safety. The other boat was getting close—the spotlight beam swept back and forth, searching. I was freaked out of my mind!

Kicking away from the *Amor*, I sailed out over the

waves. I flinched, then cut deep into the freezing waters of the Pacific.

Surfacing, I gasped for air. Wiping salty water from my eyes, I watched the spotlight play across the command bridge of the *Amor de Cosmos*. The other boat moved closer to the *Amor*; on its deck was a young man.

Whatever he held was on fire. A bottle stuffed with a flaming rag? Then I understood. *A Molotov cocktail*, I thought. *There's gasoline in that bottle*.

The weapon flew through the air, smashing on the deck of our boat. Almost immediately, it began to burn. Flames licked greedily across the hardwood. From the *Outlaw*, a voice called, "Don't mess with me."

As the *Outlaw* powered away, I started swimming toward shore. I was so cold, but I forced myself to keep moving. Seawater was in my eyes and getting down my throat, but finally I stumbled up a rocky beach. Tiffany and Paris were hiding behind a bush. Tiffany waved me over; her teeth were chattering.

"Are you okay?" I asked anxiously.

"Sure, I'm just so cold . . ."

Paris had his arms around Tiffany. "That's one serious dude. We were lucky to get out alive." His sombre eyes gazed across the water. Orange and red flames were eating into the wooden deck and up the deck-house of the *Amor de Cosmos*. The fire spread quickly; black smoke smeared the stars.

"What would my dad say?" Paris groaned.

Tiffany squeezed his hand.

I looked at Paris. "Do you think that guy was planning a break-in at your estate?"

He nodded. "That's probably it."

On the sea, flames chased each other across the doomed vessel. They were reflected in the eyes of Paris deMornay. "I can't believe what I'm seeing. The *Amor* is finished."

"Honey, we're safe," Tiffany said gently. "That's what matters. The *Amor de Cosmos* was only a boat."

"Sure," Paris said, hanging his head. "But it was my father's boat."

* * *

The next evening, thunder boomed and lightning exploded across the sky. What drama! I was at Thirteen Oaks, sitting with Tiffany, Paris, and Paris's younger brother, Hart, on stone benches in the garden. We were watching an awesome light show illuminate the dark ocean waters. So far, rain had not fallen.

"Thunderstorms are unusual for Victoria," said Hart deMornay, smiling at me. Hart was 20, and there was also a younger teenage sister named Pepper. These were the deMornays; their parents' death had left them a large fortune that was controlled by a family trust.

Hart had luminous grey eyes and chestnut-brown hair; a lock fell across his lightly freckled face. He seemed really West Coast, like he'd been hiking through forests and windsurfing since childhood—which was true. "Wow," Hart exclaimed as a lightning bolt shot down, scattering bright colours across the sea. "What a spectacle."

"Here comes the rain," Paris said, as large drops

pattered on the leaves above us. "Let's make a run for the house. Dinner will be served soon."

As we approached the front door, Paris signalled to a servant who stood waiting. Immediately the heavy wooden entrance swung open, and we all rushed inside. I was beside Tiffany, who was beautiful as always. My friend closely resembled Grace Kelly, the movie star who became a famous princess; all Tiff needed was a sparkling diamond tiara on her blonde head—and she'd probably get one as a wedding gift from her wealthy dad.

Tonight Paris was very stylish, wearing a white dress shirt and pleated light wool trousers. "What's the story on your estate?" I asked him. "It's an amazing place."

"This part of Victoria is called the Uplands," he explained. "It's super classy. One of my ancestors built this big old mansion. The deMornays are a famous family in Britain. My great-grandfather came out to Canada and made a fortune."

"Your name sounds French."

"Maybe"—Paris shrugged—"but I'm British aristocracy. If I lived in England, people would call me Lord Paris deMornay. Impressive, eh?"

"I saw the story in today's *Times Colonist* about your boat going down. I hope the police find that guy."

"The chances are slim," Paris replied. "A high-speed boat like the *Outlaw* would be difficult to capture."

We were walking along a wide hallway past old-fashioned furniture and oil portraits of the deMornay ancestors. What a gloomy bunch. Then I heard the opening notes of "Jingle Bells." Paris grabbed his cell phone, and fell back to answer. The others kept walking, but I hesitated. I remembered the phone call to the *Amor*. Some might call me nosy, but it comes with the territory. I was born to be a detective.

"I'll join you later," I whispered to Tiffany.

Pretending to adjust my shoe strap, I glanced at Paris as he listened to the person who had called. A frown creased his face. "I'll call you back," Paris said, snapping shut the phone.

Paris disappeared through a doorway. I counted to 10, then followed. Finding stairs, I climbed up past cold cement walls. In the upper hallway, small yellow lights gleamed above the oil portraits lining the walls.

I heard a voice from behind a door. It was Paris, talking on the phone. I tiptoed closer.

"Don't threaten me," I heard Paris say angrily. "You'll get every dollar, very soon. Yes, plus your exorbitant interest."

I held my breath, listening.

Then I heard a noise from down the hallway. Footsteps—someone was coming my way!

* * *

I was motionless, frozen, as a tall man approached. He wore formal clothing. His cheeks were hollow, his white hair was thin. It was Cambridge, the butler at Thirteen Oaks.

"Good evening, Miss Austen," Cambridge said with a dusty voice as he walked past.

A door opened, and Paris stared at me. The cell phone was in his hand. "Liz? Why aren't you at the dining room?"

"I . . . I'm lost."

"Huh?"

"I can't find my room."

Paris shook his head, looking impatient. "There's a map of Thirteen Oaks. Ask Pepper for a copy."

"Is that your office?" I asked, looking at the room behind Paris. "May I take a look?"

"Sure, I suppose so." Paris closed his cell phone, not bothering to say goodbye to his caller.

Meanwhile I began looking around. A portrait of Paris's father hung above the desk; clearly he'd once been handsome, but in the portrait looked stern and unfriendly.

I liked the large mahogany desk and the electronic gear, but I was highly offended by the sight of real animal heads mounted on the wall. A deer, a mountain goat—even a beautiful polar bear.

"That is so depressing," I exclaimed.

Paris glanced at the heads. "Hart and Pepper don't like them, either. My father bagged those trophies. He was quite the hunter. I inherited this office from him."

"You're getting rid of them, of course."

Paris shook his head. "Not a chance. Those trophies were my dad's pride and joy."

I decided to abandon the subject—Paris could be stubborn. Instead I asked a question. "What's your job, Paris?"

"Spending my share of the family fortune. Believe me, it's a full-time occupation. The deMornay family trust has plenty in the bank. Our ancestors made big money in British Columbia from lumber and coal and fish. Back then, the pickings were easy. Unions were weak or non-existent. We got rich."

I looked at the wastebasket, which contained a bunch of ripped-up lottery tickets. "How's your luck?"

"Not good, but my horoscope predicts a big win soon." Paris looked at me. "Tiffany says you're into arts."

I wondered if he was changing the subject.

Then I nodded. "I've learned some martial arts. Occasionally they come in handy."

"No, I mean stuff like painting. The Group of Seven and other famous artists."

"We studied those guys in school," I replied, "but I can't say I'm an expert."

"Care to see a unique treasure?"

"Sure thing."

At the ground floor we followed a long hallway. "I haven't been in this wing of the house," I told Paris.

He smiled. "It would take days to explore Thirteen Oaks. It's a big place—but my parents were happy here."

"Hey," I exclaimed, "what's with the laser beams?" We stopped at the door of a large library. Red beams, pencil-thin, shone from wall to wall.

"Any intruder steps into here," Paris said, "and the beams trigger alarms everywhere."

"What are you protecting?"

"Can I swear you to secrecy?"

"Of course."

Paris punched numbers on a security panel outside the library door. (I couldn't help noticing the code.)

The red beams were instantly gone, although the room still seemed to glisten with their energy.

"You've heard of the acclaimed artist Emily Carr, of course," Paris said, as we stepped into the library. As well as lots of books, there were several leather sofas and mahogany writing desks.

I nodded. "She's really famous. Every Christmas my brother and I give Mom the new Emily Carr calendar. Mom loves her paintings."

"Miss Carr was born in Victoria in 1871," Paris said, "the same year that B.C. became the sixth province of Canada. For many years she travelled British Columbia by horseback and canoe, capturing totem poles and forest scenes and First Nations communities with her artistry. It's beautiful stuff. The way she did some forests, it's like the trees are actually moving—you can feel the power of the wind. Most of those old totem poles were collected by museums, or rotted and fell down, so it's good she recorded them in their original settings."

"In grade 10 we read Emily Carr's book *Klee Wyck*," I said. "Our teacher said that means 'Laughing One.' Klee Wyck was Emily Carr's honorary name, given to her by the First Nations. Mrs. Silsbe told us the people liked Emily Carr."

Paris turned to the fireplace, where no fire burned. Above the mantel was a large oil painting. It showed totems outside wooden longhouses; I could see people chatting, and canoes pulled up on shore. In the foreground, a woman laughed heartily. Beside her was a child with solemn eyes. The woman's face was radiant with life. Printed in a corner was *M. EMILY CARR*, followed by the date *1912*.

"Is that Emily Carr? The woman in the picture?"

"No," Paris replied. "I imagine she was a resident of that village back in 1912, when Miss Carr painted this picture."

"I haven't seen it before," I said. "It's never been in Mom's calendars."

"That's because it's a secret," Paris explained. "You're looking at Emily Carr's unknown master-piece. It's called *Klee Wyck*."

"Just like her book," I commented.

Paris nodded. "Miss Carr gave the picture to my grandfather, in return for something she wanted from our family store downtown. She was usually broke—a typical artist. Her paintings didn't become really valu-able until after her death." A smirk touched his perfect lips. "Emily Carr desperately needed furniture, so Grandfather traded some junky old stuff in return for this painting. Our family did well, and no one got hurt. Thanks to my clever grandfather, we own an Emily Carr original that is unknown to art collectors. Can you imagine its value?"

"Multi gazzilions, at least," I said, shaking my head. "No wonder all the security."

"I promised my father I'd protect this painting," Paris said, "and never sell it." In the hallway he punched in the code, and the red lasers bounced back to life. "It's time to eat."

"Where's the dining room?" I asked.

"I'll lead the way," Paris responded. "This is a big old house, eh, with lots of crooked hallways. I used to explore this place with Hart and Pepper when we were kids."

We turned a corner—and the others were visible in the distance. I could see Tiffany chatting with Hart and Pepper deMornay. The dining room was like something from an old horror movie. Outside tall windows, rain lashed down on a marble statue of a Greek goddess and blew in crooked streams across the glass. Thunder crackled and lightning split the sky. Around the table were solemn servants wearing white aprons over black dresses, with white caps on their heads. They were serving food to Tiffany and the others, who sat on hard chairs at a long table surrounded by the large, dark spaces of the bleak room.

A gust of wind, smelling of the sea, guttered tall candles along the table. I hurried to join Tiffany, who was giggling with Hart deMornay, who looked *really good* by candlelight.

"Sorry I'm late," I said.

Turning to Pepper, I smiled hello. Pepper deMornay was 17, like me. She was a single parent with an 18-month-old named Amanda. Pepper's eyes were big and brown, and she was very friendly. Pepper's chestnut-coloured hair fell to her shoulders, and was beautifully cut. She wore a nice blouse, jeans, and cowboy boots.

To my right, a face leaned in. It was sad-looking Cambridge, the family butler whom I had seen earlier upstairs. Cambridge was middle-aged, but acted older. He took my order for a glass of chocolate milk, then withdrew.

We were served B.C. salmon for dinner, and it was really toothsome. Tiffany and I talked to Hart about his love of the wilderness, and I could tell that Tiff was impressed by Hart's passion for life.

Then Tiffany accidentally dropped her fork; she looked embarrassed, but I just smiled. "That means a female visitor," I told her. "If you'd dropped a knife, Thirteen Oaks could expect a male visitor."

She grinned. "Oh, Liz. You and your superstitions."

Hart turned to Paris. "There was a call from the Royal Victoria Yacht Club. Your membership payment is way overdue, but I guess that doesn't matter now."

This upset Paris, and the brothers began arguing.

As they bickered, Pepper leaned close to me and murmured, "Did you see *Klee Wyck*?"

I nodded. "How'd you guess?"

"I told Paris to show you," Pepper replied. "I figured you'd be interested. Liz, is the security code still 7-7-6-6?"

When I hesitated, Pepper grinned. "So, it is, eh? I knew you'd notice. It's about time Paris changed the code. It's been used for weeks. All the servants probably know it by now."

She stopped talking as a servant presented us with frosted silver dishes of my favourite dessert, ice cream! "Did you know," Pepper said, "that Emily Carr was profiled on *Biography* in June? They did a week of famous artists." Pepper shook her head. "I bet the value of *Klee Wyck* rises by thousands of dollars every minute."

A deep *boom-boom-boom* came from the grandfather clock in a gloomy corner. Pepper jumped and nervously checked her watch before turning to Tiffany.

"Would you hold Amanda for a while?"

"For sure."

As my friend eagerly accepted the bundle of joy,

Pepper picked up her cell phone from the table and left the dining room. I smiled at Tiffany—she seemed totally at peace whenever she cuddled Amanda. Tiff adored babies and was looking forward to starting a family.

When Pepper returned to her chair, she glanced at Paris. "You still think my idea is stupid?"

"You mean the recording studio you're going to buy? The one that's vastly overpriced?"

"I'm going to become a music producer, Paris, and you can't stop me."

"Pepper, your idea is *so* bad, I've gotta laugh. You're always talking about stuff you're going to do. First it was producing for television, then lamebrain dot-com investments. Get a grip, Pepper. You're an unwed teenaged mother. How are you going to be a successful producer?"

"I'll have the money soon," Pepper declared. "You wait and see."

Hart leaned forward to squeeze her hand. "Personally, sis, I like your idea a lot. You could do anything, you're that smart."

Pepper blushed. "Thanks," she said, smiling shyly.

Tiffany looked at her fiancé. "Please stop arguing with Pepper and Hart, okay? Lately there's so much yelling. My nerves can't take it."

Pepper looked at her brother with hostility. "Ever since Mom and Dad died, you've been different. You're so crabby and jittery. Your friends were always phoning, and now you sit alone. What happened to all your snowboarding pals? When your money dried up, they did, too?"

Paris slammed his hand against the mahogany table. "Mind your own business, Pepper. Just leave me alone, okay?"

Standing up, he hurried from the room. Tiffany immediately went after him, and I followed. I found my friend in a dark hallway, staring moodily at the portraits lit by small lights. "Where'd Paris go?" I asked.

Tiffany shook her head. "He's disappeared. This old mansion is full of secret passages, and the deMornays know them all."

"Secret passages? Really?"

"That's what Pepper was saying."

"Tiff, *is* Paris different these days?"

"Sure, Liz, but he's under tremendous pressure. Cut him some slack, okay?"

"I'll try my best, Tiff," I replied, vowing to refrain from further comment.

We wandered in silence through the gloomy old mansion, and then I grabbed Tiffany by the arm. "Look," I whispered.

In the distance was the library, home to the highly prized painting by Emily Carr. But something was wrong—we couldn't see the lasers that provided security for the artwork.

Then a flashlight beam cut the darkness inside the library. It flickered and flashed—a spooky image. Next we saw a young man step into the hallway. He wore black jeans, a jacket, and a woollen cap. Two golden hoops glittered in his right ear.

He was carrying the painting.

3

Glancing at Tiffany, I put a warning finger to my lips as we shrank back against the wall. My heart was pounding overtime—what if the guy heard us?

Kneeling down in the hallway, he swiftly removed the painting from its frame. He used some kind of staple remover; each *kachunk* was a scary sound, echoing past us. Rolling up the painting, the intruder quickly slipped it inside a large metal tube. Then he was gone, disappearing down a hallway. It was all over in seconds.

Tiff stared at me in horror. "Liz, what should we do? Paris is going to be *freaked*. That painting meant everything to his father."

"Okay, Tiff, take it easy. Let's follow that guy."

Was this crazy? I wasn't sure, but my friend was highly agitated and I wanted to help. "This way," I said, leading Tiffany along the shadowy hallway. From the distance came sounds; we followed for what seemed an eternity. Down one hallway we went, then another.

Eventually we felt fresh air on our faces and smelled the ocean. We reached an open door—outside, the rain was pouring down. A concrete path led to the nearby shore, where I saw an old wharf. On the sea was a boat I recognized. It was the *Outlaw*.

Almost for sure, the stolen painting was on board.

As the vessel raced away into the night, Tiffany stared after it. She looked so sad. "We've lost the Emily Carr. I can't believe this has happened."

* * *

Tiffany and I were silent as we returned to the library. The laser beams remained down, their mission in ruins. The others had discovered the theft and were standing outside the library. Hart, Pepper, Paris, even Cambridge and several servants—they all clustered around us. Everyone kept saying, *What happened . . . What happened*? Paris was so upset; he didn't say a word, but his fists were curled up hard.

The abandoned frame lay in the hallway outside the library. "Don't touch the frame," I warned. "The police will want to dust it for fingerprints. That thief wasn't wearing gloves."

Paris started to speak, then changed his mind.

Everyone was glum as we went into the library. I looked at the large empty space above the mantel, then turned to the circle of watching faces. "This was an inside job," I declared. "Someone helped that thief."

Hart stared at me. Then he asked Cambridge to bring some coffee to the library.

"Have you called the police?" I asked Paris.

He gazed into the empty fireplace. "No."

"But why?" I asked.

"The police weren't called because we don't want publicity. No one knows about our painting—and that's how it stays. This information stays inside the family."

"I know about it."

"Sure, because you're my fiancée's best friend and you're trustworthy. No one else must learn the secret."

I was amazed at such foolishness. Without police help, the family might never recover the *Klee Wyck*. I turned to the others, expecting astonishment equal to mine. But no one cared. Pepper looked bored and Hart was whispering something to Tiffany.

Then Tiff looked at me. "I agree with Paris. We must protect our families—that's what counts the most."

Not impressed, I shook my head at their folly. Paris smiled, obviously pleased that he'd demonstrated who was boss at Thirteen Oaks.

* * *

Tiffany and I left the library, heading for our rooms.

"Paris really should call the police," I commented. "After all—"

"Let's trust him," Tiff snapped. "Paris knows what he's doing."

"Okay," I replied. "I didn't mean to upset you."

"Don't worry about it, Liz. I'm just on edge."

We stood for a moment outside Tiffany's bedroom. "Lock your door," I urged her. Tiff smiled at me with huge angel eyes. She seemed so fragile, like the famous Tiffany glass designs that share her name.

"I like Hart," I said. "He's nice."

She smiled. "That guy has so much energy."

Saying goodnight, I opened the door to my bedroom. The storm was over. Bright moonlight shone through the tall windows, glinting from the crystal angel I'd hung there.

Crossing the large room, I looked at the midnight garden. The radiance of the silver moon filled the sky, spreading a shining lustre over bushes and trees. A driveway curved past rolling lawns toward the estate's main gate. Somewhere in the night a vehicle passed on Beach Drive; I heard its tires on the wet pavement, but tall trees hid it from view.

I yawned hugely—what an evening. Going into the bathroom, I brushed and flossed at the marble sink while thinking about the mansion's strange inhabitants. Wearing my favourite PJs, I crawled into the big four-poster bed, made notes about the case, and then fell sound asleep.

* * *

Up early the next morning, I went outside. The first gentle rays of sunshine lit the garden leaves, green and wet with dew. The grass was so beautiful—it looked like velvet. The garden was filled with honeyed scents.

Surrounded by roses and sweet honeysuckle, I

wandered through the gardens of the estate, then approached the ocean. The sea air was delicious—I snuffled the morning breezes like a cat and let sunshine warm my face.

"Hi there."

Turning, I saw Hart deMornay climbing a path from the shoreline below. His face was radiant. Grinning at me, Hart swept back a lock of wavy brown hair. Beyond him, sunshine sparkled on the ocean, where seagulls swooped and played.

"I was out in my kayak," Hart explained. "Hey, Liz, you look all sunshine and happiness."

"Thanks." I was pleased. "Actually, I've been feeling down."

"Because of the robbery?"

"I guess so."

"You're a private eye type, eh? Got any theories?"

I studied Hart's large eyes and pleasant face. He looked so trustworthy, and yet . . .

Then Hart spoke. "Liz, be careful. My brother has a short temper. Don't rattle him."

"Hey! Paris and I are best buddies."

"Maybe once," Hart said with a smile. "But not now."

Opening the door of a small shed, he stowed the kayak's paddle inside. I looked at the scuba gear on the walls. "Look at this stuff!"

"All my family scuba," Hart told me. "Pater taught us."

"Who?"

Hart grinned. "*Pater* means 'father' in Latin. It's a snobby way of saying Daddy, and my father was a snob. Worse, he was a rich snob." Hart glanced suddenly at me. "When the *Amor de Cosmos* was firebombed, did you recognize the person who threw the Molotov cocktail?"

"No," I replied.

"Are you sure?"

"Of course," I said, smiling. "I'm very observant."

"Because—"

A screen door slammed, then Pepper appeared on the porch with her baby. Pretty in pink, Amanda looked so cute in her mother's arms. "Hey, you two," Pepper said, "come for breakfast. Liz, please tell me again about the werewolf in New Brunswick. I like that story."

"Okay." I grinned. "But this will be the third time."

"I'll join you shortly," Hart said. "I've got an important phone call to make."

Pepper and I ate in a pleasant sunroom overlooking both the ocean and the driveway. Just offshore was the small island I'd noticed before, its many trees emerald green in the morning sunshine. "I'd love to explore that island," I said. "Is there a rowboat or something I could use to get there?"

Pepper surprised me with a warning. "Stay away from that island, Liz. During the last war it was used by the army for training exercises. There are unexploded bombs and mines, all over the place."

"Are you certain?"

"Of course. It's called Hidden Island. I know everything about Thirteen Oaks. I'm totally into the past, just like Hart." She paused, thinking. "I guess we're both curious, like our mom. She was always talking history." Pepper sighed. "I wish I'd lived back when Thirteen Oaks was built. All that luxury, and all those parties. Sometimes, these days, I get so bored."

* * *

Arriving at the sunroom, Hart poured us all a glass of organic apple juice. It was some good. As I was downing a second glass, we heard a car stop outside.

"It's Laura," Pepper said, immediately leaving the room.

"What a car," I exclaimed, gazing out the window at a top-of-the-line BMW. Behind the steering wheel was a woman in her 30s; her auburn hair was stylishly swept back from an intelligent face with large, expressive eyes. Her makeup was immaculate. "I told Tiffany there'd be a female guest," I said, smiling at Hart.

"That's our family lawyer," Hart said. "Her name is Laura Singlehurst. Laura is responsible for the family trust. All the expenses at Thirteen Oaks are paid by the trust, and we each receive a large allowance." Hart glanced at me. "I don't need extra money—I own a company that does well in ecotourism. So I donate my allowance to the Hospice Society."

"Laura looks so interesting," I said, as the lawyer stepped from her elegant vehicle. From the colour of her car to her earrings, dress, and shoes, Laura was totally coordinated. Everything was the same lovely shade of green.

"Laura's very pleasant," Hart said. "I like her, and Pepper does, too. Laura's kind of a mother figure—if someone that glamorous can be called Mom." Hart chuckled. "But Paris hates Laura because she refuses to increase his allowance. You've heard that a fool and his money are soon parted—well, Paris is a perfect example."

As I stood up from the kitchen table, I saw Pepper approach Laura. They had a short conversation that left Pepper scowling.

"Laura didn't approve of Pepper dropping out of school because of the baby," Hart explained to me. "Sometimes Laura gets too bossy with Pepper. She can take the mother figure stuff a bit too far, if you know what I mean."

"Why don't you say something to her?"

Hart gave me a rueful smile. He swept back a lock of chestnut-coloured hair. "I guess I'm not very assertive, Liz."

Outside, the summer air was warm. Hart introduced me to Laura, who was kind and charming. We chatted about the wedding, then Laura produced a copy of the Victoria *Times Colonist*. "Look at this, Hart," she said proudly, opening to a report on the city's social scene. "I'm mentioned again today by Jim Gibson." She thrust the newspaper into Hart's hand. "Keep this copy—I've got more."

"You're always in the newspaper, Laura. With all the publicity, you'd be a natural for politics."

"Not a chance." Laura leaned on the car horn. Its sharp sound vibrated off the stone walls of the house, making birds fly up from the garden.

The sleepy face of Paris deMornay looked down

from an upstairs window. "What's with the noise?"

"Get down here fast," Laura called to him. "I've got news about your stolen painting."

Paris stared at Laura in amazement, then he disappeared from the window.

Hart's face also registered astonishment. "How'd you know the *Klee Wyck* was stolen? My brother strong-armed us into silence on that one."

The lawyer held up her cell phone. "I just had a call from some guy demanding a ransom."

"Could you identify his voice?" I asked.

Laura shook her head. "Only that he sounded young. Maybe 20 or so."

"Have you got call display?"

Laura nodded. "It said Unknown Caller. He was at a pay phone, I think. I could hear traffic sounds. Then a construction jackhammer started pounding, and he cut the connection."

Paris joined us and heard the details. "We must pay the ransom," he declared. "How much is it?"

Laura produced a pocket notebook. She'd written the ransom demand in ink the same elegant colour as her car.

When Paris saw the ransom, his face turned white. "That's . . . it's so much, I . . ."

"It's a lot," Laura agreed, "but the trust has enough money. However, that's only if you three considerably reduce your allowances for the next two years."

Paris gulped. His skin was pale, and he hadn't shaved. "We'll pay the ransom," he said at last. "That painting was Pater's favourite thing, and I just can't face losing it."

"That's okay with me," Hart said, and Pepper nodded her agreement.

"What happens next?" I asked Laura.

"I was told to expect another phone call, but I don't know when."

Paris looked at us all. "Say nothing about the painting being gone. I don't want the media to get wind of this story."

"What about the police?" I asked. "Have you changed your mind about telling them?"

"No way," Paris replied vehemently.

* * *

Later that day, Tiffany and I left Oak Bay for downtown Victoria. Her father had arrived a week earlier from Winnipeg and was staying at the world-famous Empress Hotel. He was treating us to the hotel's celebrated Afternoon Tea at four o'clock.

Tiffany drove a candy-apple red Jeep, open to the sky. On the radio aerial, a Canadian flag whipped back and forth. The air was sweet as we zoomed along Rockland Avenue, Tiff's favourite route to downtown. Sometimes we'd detour past Craigdarroch Castle so we could gaze at the impressive setting for her forthcoming wedding.

"Victoria has police radar," I warned, noting the 30-kilometre speed limit.

As a gesture to me, Tiffany slowed down. Leafy trees shaded the road, which curved past ancient mansions featuring massive, amazing gardens. Every size of blossom seemed represented in the Rockland neighbourhood.

"Listen, Tiff," I said, "has Paris mentioned someone called Bigoted Earl?"

She nodded. "Paris often goes to Sandown to see the earl."

"What's Sandown?"

Tiffany shrugged. "I've no idea."

She glanced at her diamond—a big, honking solitaire. "The castle is up that street," she said, gesturing past the trees. "But I guess you know that."

"You always talked about a church wedding, Tiff. That was your dream."

She nodded. "Yeah, but Daddy insists on the castle for the wedding. He's showing off, I think—but what can you do?"

"I hate to repeat myself, but isn't 19 kind of young for marriage?"

Tiffany smiled comfortably. "Princess Victoria, daughter of Queen Victoria, was married at 17—"

"You've told me that, but . . ."

"In the upper classes, Liz, many young people are pledged to each other. I've known couples to marry the moment they're of legal age. That way the benefits can get started. Like combining families and fortunes, and maybe titles."

"And how do you feel about Paris? Still happy?"

Tiff produced a smile of sweet innocence. "Paris loves me, Liz. Since I was 12, I knew I really did want to marry him. We're so good together—and we understand each other." Her voice trailed off, and she frowned. Then she seemed to shake off her thoughts. "Anyway," she said brightly, "we've been through the same fires growing up. Both our fathers demanded a lot of us, right from childhood. It turned into a terrible burden for Paris. He could never meet his father's expectations. I understand that, and I help Paris with his feelings. He really needs me."

"What do *you* need, Tiff?"

She shrugged. "To have a family, and to know my parents are okay."

"What about college or university? You're very bright. You could have a career."

"I've got a lifetime supply of money, Liz. I don't need a career. I want my very own babies, a real family, and then I'm going to establish a charitable foundation. I'll help children, especially in war zones."

The Jeep hung a left, and we moved south under leafy boughs. In Cook Street Village the chestnut trees were glorious, shading little shops and wide sidewalks where people read newspapers outside coffee shops and lovers kissed.

As we approached the ocean I began to notice the wind, how it bent trees low. I saw whitecaps out on the sea racing toward shore.

"It's a windstorm," Tiff said. "Let's go watch."

She followed Dallas Road to St. Charles, where we found parking. "Hart brought me here during a storm," Tiffany said, as we left the Jeep. "It was so awesome. The waves were, like, huge."

The white buildings along the seashore reminded me of the Mediterranean, and so did the sea. The breakers were blue and green, tossed and turbulent. Spray flew away as they pounded ashore, noisily rattling stones when the waters ran back into the sea. In the distance, wave after wave crashed on the stony beach and came racing toward us along the shoreline.

I noticed that police had set up a roadblock, preventing vehicles from using this section of Dallas Road during the storm. Huge waves crashed against the concrete roadway, scattering ocean foam and seawater across the pavement.

I looked at the far side of the roadway. "What's there?"

"Ross Bay Cemetery. Cambridge told me it's the oldest burial ground in the city. Some famous people are in it, like Emily Carr."

"Wow," I suddenly exclaimed, pointing at the ocean pounding the roadway. "Look at that *vision*."

Out of the waves came a blond runner, a tall guy in his late teens. Head down, he plunged through the cascading waves with total determination. He was soaked but he kept moving.

"He's really something," I said, watching as the runner stopped at a small low-rider truck parked nearby on St. Charles. The windows were tinted; I couldn't see the driver. "Maybe that truck's from Seattle."

"How come?"

"It's got a Washington plate."

Tiff smiled. "You're so observant."

"I forgot my camera," I replied, "and I regret my foolishness. I could use a photo of that dreamboat. Maybe he's in movies. Lots of shows get made in B.C."

"Put that guy on the screen and he'll be the next big thing."

A window rolled down. I couldn't see the driver,

but it seemed he was speaking to the blond guy. Then the runner was handed a wad of bills. After carefully counting the money, he disappeared up St. Charles. The truck also took off. I never got a look at the driver.

4

Soon after, Tiffany parked the Jeep near downtown on Burdett. This was a pleasant street of apartment buildings and dignified mansions dominated by a massive cathedral. As Tiffany snapped a locking device on the steering wheel, I nodded my approval.

Sunlight filtered down through the leaves. A clergyman riding an old bicycle waved hello, and a young mother pushing a baby carriage smiled at us. "It's a friendly town," I commented to Tiffany, as we walked to Fort Street for some shopping on Antique Row.

Our mission was to purchase gifts for the wedding party, then meet Tiffany's dad for Afternoon Tea at the Empress Hotel. Many of the storefronts made me think of Olde England, back in the days of Scrooge and his creator, Charles Dickens. Displayed in windows along the street were many treasures, from antique jewellery to the finest furniture.

In a jewellery shop, Tiffany studied two large buttons on display. "Objects are different when they're old," she said. "These buttons are so heavy, eh? I bet they're from a soldier's uniform, back in the First World War."

Tiff studied the Latin inscription on the buttons. "You know something, Liz? I have a real emotional affinity for those times. Even when I was very small I was fascinated by images from the days of the British Empire." Tiffany paused. "If ever I lived before," she said, "it was then."

Back outside, we wandered past an upscale auction house. "Look at these classic train sets," I said, stopping at the window. "My brother Tom would love this place—"

"Liz, look!" Tiffany pointed into the auction house. "That painting—it's Lady deMornay. But I saw it at Thirteen Oaks, just days ago. It was in the morning room. That's where Lady deMornay used to sit, watching the sea."

Tiffany snapped open her miniaturized cell phone. "Hello, Paris?" she said, moments later. "Listen, that portrait of your mother has maybe been stolen. Liz and I just spotted it, up for auction."

As she listened to Paris, Tiffany frowned. "But she's your own mother, Paris. How could you auction her portrait? Hart and Pepper will be devastated." Tiffany kept talking, then stared at the phone.

"He hung up on me."

I started to comment, then pointed in the window of the auction house. "Tiffany, look who's in there."

"Oh, gosh—it's Cambridge, the butler."

"See how he's staring at the portrait of Lady deMornay? Like he's going to start crying."

We watched Cambridge for a few minutes, but nothing much happened. I felt impatient to do something—to make progress on this case. Opening a map of Victoria, I located the Maritime Museum. "We could check their records for information about the *Outlaw*. Like who's the owner and where it's registered."

"Sure, let's try that," Tiffany immediately replied. "Anything to find the painting. Paris was in a really bad mood this morning."

* * *

Without highrise towers to block the sun, the downtown streets were bright and attractive. They were crowded with tourists and shoppers and office workers. People looked so fit and healthy!

"Look at that crow," I said, pointing. It had landed on a bicycle that leaned against a lamp standard; in the bicycle basket was a shopping bag containing bagels. The crow took a bagel, then lifted off with it.

"Stop, thief," Tiffany called, laughing.

At Bastion Square we found a lively street market with booths selling artwork and wonderful crafts. I got started on my own gift list by finding something pretty for my mom (earrings made of cobalt-blue glass beads), then we went inside the Maritime Museum.

With luck, we happened to meet the museum's director, a nice woman named Yvonne. "We're looking for information about a boat called the *Outlaw*," I said.

"Can you help?"

"Perhaps," Yvonne said. "Let's try the library."

She escorted us into an unusual elevator. "This is the oldest operating birdcage elevator in Canada," Yvonne told us.

The double metal doors clanked closed, and our birdcage began to rise. I grinned. "This is cool."

At the top floor, Yvonne opened the elevator door. "There are some beautiful old buildings in Victoria, many dating back to the gold rush. This one is from the 19th century; it used to be the courthouse. You've heard of Matthew Begbie?"

We both shook our heads.

"They called him the Hanging Judge because of the number of people he sentenced to die. This is the actual building where he presided."

The ceiling of the library was high; above us, portraits of British royalty were displayed beside the Canadian coat of arms. "You know something I like about Victoria?" I said. "All the connections to England. Like those British candy shops we've seen."

The museum's librarian, Lynn, was smart like Yvonne. Diligently searching the archives and photo files, they managed to discover one vessel named the *Outlaw*. "It's listed in *Lloyd's Register* of ships," Yvonne said, studying a thick volume. "But it can't be your *Outlaw*. This one's a freighter, built in 1946 for general cargo and registered in Malta. I'm sorry, I guess you're out of luck. Probably the boat you're seeking has never been registered. It's an *Outlaw*, just like its name implies."

I smiled at them. "Thanks, anyway, for trying."

In the hallway we stopped at an original poster from 1911 showing the *Titanic* and her sister ship, the *Olympic*. A shiver went through me, thinking of the iceberg and that horrifying night.

Inside the birdcage elevator again, we descended noisily to the ground floor, where Yvonne introduced us to a bearded man named Richard, who also worked there. Richard wore a tie displaying nautical flags, and he was an expert on matters of the sea.

"My suggestion," he said, after hearing our story, "is to visit Fishermen's Wharf. Ask for Fossilized Pete. If anyone's heard of the *Outlaw*, it'll be Pete." Richard smiled at us. "Tell you what, I'll phone Pete and set up a meeting. He's a friend of mine."

I spoke to Pete, who sounded friendly, and we arranged to meet in the early evening. After thanking Richard, we returned to Bastion Square with Yvonne, who was going on a break. Above our heads, flags fluttered in the summer breeze. A few paces from the museum, Yvonne showed us a row of bricks embedded in the pavement. "The wall of Fort Victoria was here." Yvonne looked toward the city's nearby Inner Harbour. "The fort started at the ocean and ran past us to Government Street. Things were pretty calm in Victoria until the big gold rush of 1858. Twenty thousand prospectors came through here, heading for the goldfields."

Tiffany looked at Yvonne. "We're on Vancouver Island, right? But the city of Vancouver is over on the mainland. That's, like, totally confusing."

"I agree," Yvonne said. "George Vancouver was an English sea captain who mapped the waters of the Pacific Northwest. Adding to the confusion, in Washington state there's another city named Vancouver."

"Wasn't Captain Vancouver eaten by cannibals?"

"No." Yvonne shook hands goodbye. "Look for the statue of Captain James Cook near the Empress Hotel—he once explored these waters. You'll also see Captain Vancouver, high atop the Legislative Building. And good luck in finding the *Outlaw*."

"We'll do our best," I promised her.

* * *

At Government Street a busker was thumping a guitar, while his friend sang with a powerful voice. "They're great," Tiffany exclaimed at the end of the song. She gave them a generous donation.

"Wow, thanks," the boy said, staring at the money.

The singer hugged Tiffany. "You're so cool."

"Where's the food bank?" Tiffany asked.

The singer pointed north. "It's on Queens."

Soon we reached the Mustard Seed Food Bank, which was a busy place. "There are a lot of young families," I said in dismay. "Look at all the kids. It's shocking."

"I know," Tiffany replied sadly. "It's so wrong that a country as wealthy as Canada allows children to live in poverty. It's a national disgrace."

Tiffany asked to meet the manager of the Mustard Seed, then wrote out a cheque. The manager gasped when she saw the amount Tiffany was donating. "Thank you so much. Let me show you around the premises."

As we returned to sunshine, Tiffany consulted her watch. "Time to meet Daddy."

"Will your mother be attending the wedding?" A year earlier there'd been a divorce, and Tiff's mother now lived on Grand Cayman Island.

Tiff shook her head. "For some reason she no longer approves of Paris, and she and Daddy haven't been getting along lately, so it's probably for the best."

Tiffany was looking anxiously along Johnson Street. "Oh, good—there's a Kabuki Kab."

Kabukis are popular with tourists in Victoria. You sit in a cab attached behind a bicycle, and the driver describes why he loves this city while pedalling you to a destination.

Our driver was friendly, and I enjoyed the ride. Soon we arrived at Victoria's Inner Harbour, where the waters of the Pacific reach into the heart of the city. People were posing for pictures; beyond them was the spectacular sight of the provincial Legislative Buildings, where British Columbia's government holds its meetings. Above the imposing stone walls were many green domes, the tallest topped by a golden statue of Captain Vancouver. Many other buildings overlooked the water; some were brick and stone structures still surviving from the gold rush days, but we also saw the latest in luxury condos and upscale hotels.

Plus, of course, there was the fabled Empress.

A favourite of Hollywood stars and the very wealthy, the enormous hotel dominated the scene. Its walls rose high above to a giant Canadian flag that fluttered against the blue sky.

Two friendly doormen in fancy uniforms welcomed

us to the Empress; the lobby was filled with huge bouquets of fresh flowers radiating sweet fragrances. Right away I spotted Tiff's dad, Major Wright. His skull shone beneath grey, brushcut hair; the Major was short, resembling a small bulldog in a three-piece suit as he paced back and forth while glancing impatiently at his gold watch. Tiffany's father was proud to have served in the armed forces, and still liked to be called "the Major."

"Daddy," Tiffany cried, running to her father for a hug.

They were obviously pleased to see each other. I shook hands with the Major. "Thank you for inviting us," I said. "I'm looking forward to this."

Major Wright smiled at me. "It's good to see you again, Liz."

People were lined up, waiting their turn to enjoy the ceremony of "taking tea" in the grand hotel's original tea lobby. Portraits of long-ago British monarchs were displayed against elegant wallpaper. We saw many exquisite flowers and even some genuine palm trees. Silver spoons clinked inside china cups. I could smell the delicious tea, and my mouth watered at the sight of the goodies being served.

"Look at the whipped cream," I whispered to Tiffany. "For sure I'm having crumpets with jam and *dollops* of whipped cream."

Major Wright snapped his fingers at a waiter. "We have a table reserved."

Soon we were seated under a portrait of Queen Mary, who wore many diamonds. "This hotel was named in honour of Queen Victoria," the Major told us, as our waiter poured tea from a silver pot. "She was the Empress of India."

"These cucumber sandwiches are so good," I said, then took another bite.

Major Wright beamed at his daughter. "Great news. I've sold our house in Winnipeg. I'm moving to Victoria, to be close when my grandchildren start arriving. My life has changed for the best, Tiffany, all thanks to your forthcoming marriage."

"That's nice, Daddy."

"My own little girl will soon be Lady deMornay, chatelaine of Thirteen Oaks. Liz, isn't that great?"

"Major Wright, you're an expert on titles. Why can't Hart become Lord deMornay?"

Tiffany's blue eyes darted to her father. "That's an interesting idea."

But Major Wright threw cold water on my brainwave. "The title goes automatically to the eldest son." He turned to his daughter. "Wouldn't it be something to meet the Royal Family, Tiffany?" Major Wright's eyes grew bright with excitement. "Maybe when you're Lady deMornay, royalty will visit Thirteen Oaks, and even stay with you. Wouldn't the folks back home in Winnipeg be jealous?"

"I guess so, Daddy."

"Call me a sentimental old fool, but I can't wait for your marriage. Joining together the Wrights and the deMornays is so important for both families. Your marriage to Paris will unite us with Victoria's top society. You'll be living in the Uplands, at the number one address—Thirteen Oaks."

Eventually the Major's enthusiasm ran down, and for

a while nothing more was said. We munched the goodies and sipped delicious tea. Then Tiffany took a deep
breath. "I've been thinking, Daddy, about the wedding."

"Yes?"

"Maybe I should postpone it? Even just a little bit?"
Tiffany spoke rapidly; her voice seemed breathless.
"It's just that . . ."

"Tiffany, sweetheart. What's wrong?"

"It's just that Paris, he's changed. I'm not sure . . ."

Major Wright took her hand; his eyes were as blue
as Tiff's. "Of course he's different, sweetie pie. He's
grieving for his parents. Wouldn't you be?"

"Of course, but—"

"Think about the grandchildren you and Paris will
give me. Those kids are the next generation of the
Wright and deMornay empire. With parents like you
and Paris, they can't fail." He gently touched the side
of Tiffany's face. "Think of the babies, honey. You're
going to love them so much."

"That's true, but—"

"The invitations have been sent, Tiffany, and beautiful presents have arrived. You can't return those! Besides, calling off the wedding would look bad."

I looked at him. "Other people have cancelled weddings."

"Sure, but—"

Tiffany interrupted his response. "Liz, I understand
what Daddy means. What would people think? That's
important, you know."

"If you say so," I replied.

As the Major patted Tiffany's hand, his cell phone
shrilled. He answered and spoke briefly, then looked at

us. "Good news. Paris is joining us for tea. His limousine just arrived outside the Empress."

"That's wonderful," Tiffany exclaimed. She fluffed up her blonde curls and straightened her skirt, but a frown remained on her face.

I watched Paris approach across the hardwood floor, smiling at the women who glanced his way. He wore a suit the colour of vanilla ice cream, with a beautiful shirt and a tie of blue silk. In his ear was a small golden hoop. His dark hair was swept back dramatically.

Paris shook hands warmly with the Major, then sat down beside Tiffany and gazed into her eyes. "Sweetheart, it's so good to see you."

Tiffany smiled happily. "You, too, Paris."

Paris turned to the Major. "Sir, you'll recall I put your name forward for membership in the Union Club. It's very exclusive, but I've got wonderful news. You've been accepted as a member."

"Wonderful." The Major shook hands with Paris. "You're a fine young man." Then he turned to Tiffany with a smile. "My own dear Lady deMornay. I can hardly wait."

* * *

Outside the Empress we said goodbye to Major Wright and Paris. Then, before I could speak, Tiffany raised her hand. "Please, Liz, no advice about my marriage. This is important to Daddy and it's important to me."

"Still, I'm glad you mentioned your doubts, Tiff. Maybe that got your father thinking."

After shopping in Chinatown, Tiff and I enjoyed a

tour of the Legislative Buildings. Then we returned outside to the sight of the Inner Harbour as evening came to Victoria. The distant hills were lovely, turning dark and mysterious before our eyes.

The air was warm; many people were out this early evening, strolling arm in arm or passing in horse-drawn carriages. Stopping at a low stone wall, we gazed at the vessels cruising the Inner Harbour. There were luxury yachts and sleek kayaks and noisy sea-planes, plus a large Zodiac full of tourists returning to port from a whale-watching excursion.

The setting sun glowed on a huge sign reading WELCOME TO VICTORIA. The words were made entirely of flowers. "Excuse us, girls," a man said with a drawl, "but how's about taking our picture?"

"Sure."

Through the lens of his camera, I focused on a middle-aged couple dressed in shorts and "Victoria City of Gardens" T-shirts. Beyond them was a statue of Queen Victoria, the famed British monarch who gave the city its name.

"You're from out of town?" I commented, after capturing the couple's self-conscious grins for posterity.

The man's bushy eyebrows rose high. "Now, little lady, how'd you guess?"

"It was easy." I smiled. "You're carrying a copy of *WHERE Victoria*. That's a tourist guide."

"Shucks." The man laughed. "For a moment there, I was impressed."

Tiffany shook her finger at the man, but in a friendly manner. "Now, listen up. My friend's a successful detective. She's very smart."

"Say," the lady remarked to me, "ever met Nancy Drew?"

"Not so far!"

The man photographed the nearby Royal British Columbia Museum. "We're here on business, hoping to sell this town a hockey arena. But we might just move to Canada. Shucks, the air is so clean—why, you can taste it."

"Some of those big flowers are *amazing*," his wife added, "and folks are so friendly."

The man looked at the Legislative Buildings. "That fellow on top, the gold statue. He's holding something, maybe a hockey stick. Someone said that's the legendary star Wayne Gretzky. Is it true?"

I shook my head. "That's Captain George Vancouver."

After saying goodbye, we descended stone stairs to the Lower Causeway. Here people strolled, licking cones as they watched buskers perform and sidewalk artists paint and sketch. Young kids were blowing rainbow bubbles, which drifted lazily through the warm air. This seemed like a carnival by the sea.

On enormous white yachts, boaters sat chatting in deck chairs or panned their cameras across the enchanting scene. Red and gold sunset colours reflected from the water and I could smell the salty ocean.

I consulted my watch. "It's time for our meeting with Fossilized Pete at Fishermen's Wharf. Richard at the museum suggested getting there by harbour ferry."

"There's one," Tiffany said, pointing.

The ferries were loading passengers at a nearby wooden wharf, which creaked with the movement of the sea. The ferry was so cute—it looked like a tiny tugboat. We stepped down into a small cabin, where other passengers waited for the departure. Surrounded by windows, we could see everything.

"Please let us off at Fishermen's Wharf," I asked the captain, as he took our fares.

"Going for fish and chips?"

I shook my head. "We stuffed our faces at the Empress."

"Will this ride make us seasick?" Tiffany asked.

"Not a chance," our captain replied. "The Inner Harbour is almost totally enclosed by land. It's very calm. We're also protected by the Sooke Hills." He pronounced it *Sook*, with a silent e. "The first inhabitants of those hills were the Tsouke people."

Proudly displaying the flags of B.C. and Canada, the ferry plowed a furrow of small waves as its bow cut through the water. Our relaxing journey ended at Fishermen's Wharf, where various vessels were moored along the wooden wharves. Signs at Barb's seafood stand asked customers to refrain from feeding birds. But one guy totally ignored the warning, holding a juicy morsel aloft to tempt the gulls that wheeled and screamed above.

"He'll lose a finger," I predicted, but I was wrong.

We followed a series of wharves to the home of Fossilized Pete; it resembled a tiny house, floating on the sea. There was even a picket fence.

A porthole overlooked the houseboat's tiny porch. As I leaned close, hoping to see inside, the door opened and Fossilized Pete stood before us.

I had expected a grizzled type, white whiskers and weathered skin, but instead Pete was quite young. He had large eyes like those of a puppy dog, and neatly trimmed black hair turning to grey. He wore deck shoes, faded jeans, and a T-shirt reading "TerrifVic Jazz Party." I asked about the *Outlaw*, showing him a rough drawing I'd made. Then I held my breath. Surely Fossilized Pete could help us.

To our delight, Pete nodded his head. "Yes, I've seen this craft before."

"Wonderful," we both exclaimed.

Pete pointed across the water. "Last night I spotted the *Outlaw* heading toward the West Bay Marina. You can see the marina's lights from here."

I exchanged an excited glance with Tiffany. "How do we get there?" I asked Pete.

He gestured at a small boat moored beside the wharf. "That's my skiff. Hop aboard."

"Wonderful."

Minutes later we were skimming across the water, powered by an outboard in the stern of the skiff. I felt determined, yet nervous. Suppose we found the *Outlaw*—what would happen then?

5

"I'm a volunteer with the Victoria Marine Rescue Society," Pete told us, as our boat sped across the waters. "We're out a lot, helping boaters in trouble, that sort of thing."

"How'd you get your name?" I asked. "Fossilized Pete doesn't really suit you."

"Actually it's a nickname. I don't smoke, I don't drink, I don't do drugs. For that, some people back home called me a fossil—you know, old-fashioned. So I moved to the West Coast, where people are more accepting of differences. I'm not considered a fossil now, but I've kept my nickname, just for the memories."

"What's your T-shirt about?" I asked.

"The Jazz Party is an annual event in Victoria.

People come from all over the world. I've danced to some great bands—Zydeco, swing, you name it. And I volunteer at the special Saturday party for kids."

For a time I was silent, thinking.

"Is it dangerous on the open sea?"

"Sure," Pete replied. "Especially for the dunder-heads, the ones with no training. They don't keep a weather eye out. Then suddenly they're overboard into bitterly cold water. People have died out there."

Looking down into the depths, I shivered. Night had closed around us; the breeze chilled my face. Directly ahead was the marina, where lights glowed inside houseboats and cabin cruisers. People on deck talked to each other across the water, and I could hear music and barking dogs. It was like entering a small town, afloat on the sea.

"I'll drop you here," Pete said.

"How do we get back?" I asked.

"Take a harbour ferry. They stop here."

Jumping onto a wharf, we waved goodbye to Fossilized Pete. Then we wandered around, hoping to spot the *Outlaw*. We showed the drawing to lots of people, but the search was doomed. It all seemed a big waste of time.

Until we spotted the thief.

He was on a nearby wharf. I studied his spiky bleach-blond hair and the two golden hoops in his ear. "That's him for sure."

"What'll we do?"

"Let's get closer."

Then his cell phone beeped. "Jason speaking," he

said. His voice came clearly to us. After listening to his caller, Jason nodded. "Thanks for the warning."

Jason dashed to a boathouse, opened the door, and disappeared inside. Moments later, we heard the throaty roar of a powerful engine as a cruiser appeared from the boathouse.

"Look," I cried. "It's the *Outlaw*."

* * *

Jason was inside, alone at the controls. "He's getting away," I said urgently. "Come on, let's stop him." I pointed along the wharf. "There's someone who can help."

We ran toward an open boat with an oversize outboard motor, mounted at its stern. The guy at the wheel had just started the motor when we reached him.

"Help us," I shouted. "We must stop that cruiser."

"O . . . kay," the guy replied. "Throw off the lines . . . and . . . and jump aboard."

The boat was stripped bare of seats and anything else that would slow it down. As we held tightly to a railing at the stern, it roared away from the marina. Many stars shone above. I could see the *Outlaw*, moving fast. I looked at the lights of condo towers, shining on the water, then felt our boat pick up speed. The motor was powerful; spray lashed back, soaking us. Lights blurred past—I shook saltwater out of my eyes, fighting to see.

"Hang on," Tiffany screamed, as the boat heeled to the side. Then I looked at the guy at the wheel—and understood our problem.

He was drinking from a vodka bottle, and it was almost empty.

* * *

The guy leered at us with bloodshot eyes. "Enjoying the ride, girls?" he yelled.

Laughing, he twisted the wheel. We both screamed as the boat almost overturned before the guy managed to right it.

I staggered forward, balancing myself, as the drunk twisted the wheel back and forth. "Keep back," he yelled at me.

"Be careful, Liz," Tiffany called.

We'd left the Inner Harbour behind and reached the open sea. Directly ahead was the massive bulk of the *Coho*, a large ferry carrying vehicles and passengers to Victoria. Its horn sounded a warning, startling the drunk. He weaved back and forth, holding tightly to the wheel, trying to watch the ferry and also watch me.

"Danger," I suddenly cried, pointing over his shoulder. "Right there!"

"*Huh*?" the drunk responded, turning to look.

I leapt for the wheel, determined to take control. But the drunk saw me coming and lashed out with his foot. Avoiding the kick, I hit the deck and rolled. Trying to aim another kick, the drunk accidentally released the wheel—and immediately the boat changed direction, veering sharply to starboard.

The drunk staggered, then fell. His head smacked against the deck, and he went silent. Stumbling forward, I managed to grab the wheel. Somehow I got the boat under control, and we zoomed safely away from the *Coho*.

"Is he breathing?" I yelled back at Tiffany.

"Yes, but he's out cold."

I turned the boat toward the Inner Harbour. A crisis had been averted, but I didn't feel good. Somewhere in the night, the *Outlaw* was getting away.

We'd lost our quarry.

* * *

We left the boat at a wharf near the Empress. When we walked away, the drunk was leaning against the bulkhead, head in his hands. He was groaning.

"When we get home," I said, "I'll phone the police about spotting the *Outlaw*. But I'm guessing Jason will move his boat to another location."

"I wonder who warned him about us," Tiff said.

"Good point."

A lot of young people were hanging out across the street from the Empress. One of them was Pepper. She was comforting a teenager who was crying; I saw tears on the girl's face. Nearby, three well-dressed teenagers were staring with hostility at Pepper.

As we approached, Pepper smiled. "Good to see you," she said. "Laura's arriving any minute now. She's giving me a ride home to Thirteen Oaks."

Laura's shiny BMW pulled smoothly to the curb. At the same moment, a city bus stopped nearby; Pepper escorted the forlorn girl to the bus, then waved goodbye as the bus pulled away.

We all climbed into the BMW. "Brother," Pepper

exclaimed. She was in the back; Tiffany was up front with Laura. "I hate gossip—I hate it. Words can cause so much pain."

"What happened?" I asked.

"That girl I was with—some boy started a rumour about her. He wrote lies on a wall, looking for revenge. You saw those three girls? They're treating the rumour like the truth and passing it along. I told them what I thought."

"You did the right thing," Laura said. "You didn't join the finger-pointers. The only way to stop that stuff is not to be one of the sheep. You showed courage, Pepper, giving friendship to an outcast."

"Thanks," Pepper said, looking embarrassed. "Anyway, no one tells me what to think. I make up my own mind about people."

* * *

We soon reached the Jeep. "Liz and I can drive Pepper home," Tiffany suggested to Laura. "It'll save you the trip."

Laura declined the offer. "I feel like a drive. I've worked hard today, and I need to unwind."

"Okay to go with you?" I asked Laura. "I'd like your advice about what happened tonight."

"You bet," Laura replied.

We all said good night to Tiffany, and the BMW purred smoothly away. As I gazed at the charming houses passing by, I told Laura and Pepper about the events at the West Bay Marina. "I feel like I'm getting somewhere on this case," I said.

"How so?" Laura enquired. She was remarkably beautiful.

"Well, Jason is clearly connected to the *Outlaw*, and he also stole the painting. I should tell the police, don't you think?"

As Laura pondered this, Pepper studied her face. Then Laura nodded. "Yes, do tell the police about Jason's link to the *Outlaw*. But you'd better not mention the painting. That would upset Paris."

"Okay," I replied, somewhat reluctantly. "Have you heard anything about the ransom?"

She shook her head. "Nothing so far."

"Do you think the caller was Jason?"

"Probably," Laura said. "You're a good detective, Liz."

I grinned. "Sleuthing's in my blood. My mom's a lawyer, just like you. She loves it."

"I went into law to have a career," said Laura. "That way I'd never be financially dependent on anyone else."

The BMW rolled quietly through the deeply shadowed streets of the Uplands district, until it reached the stone walls of the Thirteen Oaks estate. Stepping out of the luxurious car, I sniffed the fragrant breezes.

Laura waved to us from behind the wheel. "Goodnight, girls."

"Goodnight, Laura," I said. "Thanks for the ride."

The lights of the beemer disappeared into the night, and we entered the quiet gardens of the estate. The moon was lovely, and so were the glorious stars that twinkled across the heavens. "It's so perfect under the moon," I exclaimed to Pepper. "I love this place."

* * *

The next morning, Tiff and I wandered together through the gardens of Thirteen Oaks.

The garage stood at the edge of the estate. Cambridge was shining the chrome on the family limousine. The vehicle sparkled in the morning sunshine. It was a Daimler, manufactured in England. It had right-hand drive and a cream and navy two-tone finish—very nice indeed.

"The Daimler's for sale," Cambridge told us. "Master Paris has ordered me to spiff it up. He's ordered a new limousine from Detroit—it's got bulletproof glass."

"Where's the chauffeur?" Tiffany asked.

"He's quit, miss. A disagreement with Master Paris."

Cambridge then began talking about the Moss Street Paint-In. "Are you going?" he asked. "It's a famous event in Victoria, and very popular."

"What's it about?" Tiffany asked.

"All along Moss Street, local artists set up their easels. You can watch them painting, or ask questions. I go every year." For a moment Cambridge stared at the ground. "When I was young, I dreamed of being an artist. I had real talent—but it didn't work out."

"Do you still paint?" I asked.

"Oh, yes, miss. I have a small studio above the garage."

"May we visit sometime?" I asked.

Cambridge shook his head. "I don't like people to look at my work. It's . . . Well . . . Well, I do it because

. . ." His voice faded away, then he straightened up. "You'll see some good work today at the Paint-In. I suggest that you go."

* * *

It was a beautiful Saturday, and sunshine warmed our faces as we headed south in the Jeep on Beach Drive, admiring the view. Yards in the Uplands were big, big, big, and featured beautiful trees and flowering bushes, a lot of them taller than people. The hollyhocks were particularly sensational with their fat blossoms of pink and dark red. The careful landscaping in the Uplands was so elegant— many houses seemed to be set into nests of greenery. Big trees shaded us from the sun; south of Willows Beach we passed Glenlyon-Norfolk School, located beside the ocean. "According to Pepper," Tiffany said, "that place was originally a private home owned by a famous architect named Francis Rattenbury. He ended up murdered."

I stared at the building. "I wonder if there's a ghost."

"Probably not. The murder happened in England."

At Windsor Park we paused to watch a cricket match, then headed for town by way of Oak Bay Village. What a great place. The village totally reminded me of England, with its little shops selling chocolates and flowers and other delights.

One place was called the Blethering Place Tea Room. "What's a blethering place?" I wondered aloud.

"That's a Scottish expression," Tiffany explained. "It's a place where people gather for gossip and good food."

"Hey, we could ask people there if they know any-thing about the *Outlaw*."

Tiffany smiled. "Instead of always investigating, Liz, you could help me relax. I am getting so nervous. My wedding is exactly one week away."

People on the sidewalk watched us pass in the red Jeep, and then a beautifully dressed white-haired lady waved, and I returned her sweet smile. She was with a younger woman in an elegant outfit.

"This is a very nice area," I said, then turned to Tiffany to discuss something that had been on my mind. "I've been thinking—maybe Cambridge has been steal-ing artwork from Thirteen Oaks. He's got a background as an artist, so he'd know the value of the stuff."

"But Cambridge has been with the family forever. Why would he do something like that?"

I shrugged. "Could be he needs the money." It was amazing what people would do for money, I'd learned in my years of investigating.

Soon we reached Dallas Road, where a sleek cruise ship moved splendidly past on the sparkly blue ocean. In the distance, the snow-capped Olympic Mountains added grace and majesty to the scene. It was hard to believe that so recently we'd faced danger on those same waters.

Parking spots near Moss Street were at a premium, but Tiffany deftly manoeuvred the Jeep into a tiny place. Jumping out, we gazed at a welcoming scene. Sunshine splattered down through leafy trees—all along the street, artists were at work, while spectators strolled from easel to easel, sculpture to sculpture.

The atmosphere was pleasant. A girl with a French

horn played a love song, while young children passed by, their faces painted to resemble clowns and cats. The houses had wonderful gardens—one place reminded me of Snow White. Somehow I could just picture her, looking down from the tiny upstairs window with its leaded-glass panes and little curved roof.

After wandering for a while, we purchased lemonade from some kids and then joined a crowd watching a woman at work on her canvas. "The painting must have movement," she explained to us. "Without movement, art is nothing."

A yellow butterfly drifted past. I watched its serene passage through the warm air—then stared in shock.

"Tiff," I exclaimed. "Look who it is."

* * *

"It's him," Tiffany said. "From the storm."

We'd last seen this guy running through the waves as they crashed ashore on Dallas Road. He was one of the artists, and sat working on a canvas. His work was certainly impressive; several large canvases of B.C. scenery were on display. My personal favourite showed emerald forests sweeping down through a mountain valley. I longed to visit that place.

"How much?" I asked, smiling at the handsome blond artist.

He grinned. "For you, it would cost nothing. But unfortunately, it's from my private collection. This one's not for sale."

"My name is Liz," I said, "and this is my best friend, Tiffany Wright."

"I'm William. It's nice to know you."

"Well," I said reluctantly, "we'd better move along. I'm sure other fans want to talk with you."

"Hey, don't go." William studied me with his large, green eyes. "You know, my cousin has been showing my art today. I've been at my studio, working on a rush assignment—for real money, I might add. Anyway, I'm just here for an hour while my cousin gets a break. Luckily, it's the hour when you passed by."

I blushed.

"We're from Winnipeg," Tiffany explained to William, "but I'll be living here now. I'm getting married at Craigdarroch Castle."

"That's a cool place for a wedding." William turned to me. "It's totally out of the Victorian age. It's got stained-glass windows and a tower with an unforgettable view of the city. Hollywood producers have used the castle in some movies. The ballroom dancing in *Little Women*, for example."

"With Winona Ryder?"

"That's the one."

I examined William's artistry with admiration. "You're really talented. But you're, like, so young."

He smiled shyly. "My teacher says I have a gift, but I need to work, work, work. It's difficult, you know, trying to be an artist and also earn a living. When I'm not painting I'm on a Kabuki Kab, earning money for art lessons and supplies."

William told us about his admiration for Emily Carr. "My teacher is an expert on her," he explained. "Robert says some of Victoria is essentially unchanged from the days when Emily Carr lived here. You can walk the same streets, paint the same scenes."

I was dying to tell William about the theft of Emily Carr's unknown masterpiece from Thirteen Oaks, but of course I couldn't. Instead I asked, "What's her art worth?"

"Plenty," William replied. "There was an auction recently for one of her pieces called *War Canoes*, *Alert Bay*. It fetched more than a million dollars."

"Yikes."

"For more than 20 years Emily Carr struggled to earn money, and had little time for her art. She raised sheepdogs and operated a small apartment house."

William told us about Emily Carr's monkey named Woo, and how she'd take Woo for walks in a baby carriage. "Some people called her eccentric—but artists can be difficult to understand. Our challenge is to capture the essence of life, and that's a tall order."

"You're passionate about it," I said.

"Liz, my art is everything." Then William smiled. "Perhaps I'll see you again." He scribbled his phone number on a piece of paper. "Call me sometime, okay?"

"Sure," I replied, feeling amazed and happy.

Walking on, Tiff and I discussed William in detail. "He's going to be famous," I predicted. Then I grabbed Tiffany's arm. "Look, there's Hart. Who's his pretty friend?"

"I don't know." Tiff stared daggers in her direction. "Hart told me there's no one special in his life."

I glanced at Tiff. "You sound miffed."

"I doubt it."

"Methinks the lady doth protest too much."

Spotting us, Hart hurried over. "Tiff and Liz, please meet my cousin, Lorna Taft—she's arrived early for the wedding. Lorna's from Terrace, in northern B.C."

"Your cousin?" Tiff said, sounding relieved.

"Is the north a cool place to live?" I asked.

"You bet," Lorna laughed. "Especially in January."

I noticed a warm smile pass between Hart and Tiff. "We're going to visit Craigdarroch Castle," Hart explained.

Lorna nodded. "I want to see the castle where you're getting married, Tiffany."

"Come with us," Hart suggested. "The castle's a short walk from here."

"We'd love to go with you," Tiffany responded with great enthusiasm.

Chatting together, we walked through the festive Rockland neighbourhood. Every type had come for the Paint-In: grandmas and grandpas, parents and kids, yuppies and hippies, all having fun. Passing by the elegant houses, I daydreamed about being a famous artist who lived in Victoria and was adored by all.

Then the castle appeared, looming high above us. "The castle's Scottish name means 'Rocky Oak Place,'" Hart explained to us. "It was built for a man who got rich operating coal mines. Back then, the castle was surrounded by 28 acres of meadows with many Garry oaks and an artificial lake. It must have been so beautiful."

"The castle's still impressive," I said, staring at the

granite walls and tall chimneys. I could just imagine a princess brushing her hair at one of the arched windows, or gazing down at her curly-haired swain from a balcony far above.

"It's like we're in Scotland. I love the red-tiled roof."

We purchased admission tickets, then stepped into the opulent luxury of the Victorian era. Ahead was an enormous sandstone fireplace; a scene was carved inside. "Those are players in an opera by Wagner," Hart told us. "Much of the castle remains exactly the same as when the Dunsmuirs lived here. Just imagine—this place has 17 fireplaces."

"A life of abundance," his cousin commented.

Hart nodded. "The Victorians lived in a luxurious world of leather-bound books, Tiffany paperweights, stained-glass windows, and pianos by Steinway."

A wooden staircase spiralled above us to an alcove, where I could see a bouquet of flowers on an organ under a stained-glass window. "My father admires James Dunsmuir," Tiffany told us, "because of the power and prestige he commanded. That's why Daddy insists that I get married in Dunsmuir's castle." Her red lips pouted. "I was hoping for a church."

Tiff turned to me. "One of James Dunsmuir's daughters had 30 bridesmaids and flower girls—there's a picture upstairs of her wedding day."

Next we studied the drawing room. It featured a lovely chandelier, its crystals glittering blue like the sea and red like the most exquisite of rubies. In exactly one week Tiffany would be married here; the ceremony was planned for the evening, after the castle had closed to the public. Not for the first time, a wave of uneasiness passed over me as I thought of the wedding.

6

That evening Paris and Tiffany went out for supper. I summoned my courage and phoned William. My heart was beating hard, and I hoped I wouldn't sound too anxious.

To my relief, William was happy to hear from me. "I was just reading the newspaper," I said, my voice trembling. "There's a special lantern ceremony tonight. It starts at eight." I took a deep breath. "Care to go with me?"

"You bet," William replied. "I've been working hard and I could use a break."

"Wonderful."

We arranged to meet at a bus stop on Toronto Street in the James Bay neighbourhood. Stepping from the bus, I saw William waiting. He wore a "Kabuki Kabs"

T-shirt and long khaki shorts, and had a string of small shells around his neck. It felt so good to see him.

We walked south on Government Street, getting to know each other. "I've been worried about my mom," William told me. "Lately her bronchitis is so bad. I want Mom to spend time in Arizona, because of the dry air." William smiled happily. "The project I'm working on will pay for getting her to Arizona for the winter. What a relief."

We were walking past wooden houses that dated back to pioneer days. We admired the gingerbread decorations on Emily Carr's childhood home, then watched tourists pass in a graceful carriage pulled by a big horse.

"What's the story on this lantern ceremony?" William asked.

"It's apparently a tradition that began in Japan," I replied. "People are launching lanterns in paper boats to honour those who died when nuclear weapons ended the last world war."

"Now I remember—I heard about this on the radio. The boats are released on the water, while everyone prays for world peace. Right?"

I nodded. "It sounds very moving."

A lot of people had gathered beside a large, round pond. Many kids were there, carrying paper boats they'd made. A swallow darted past, moving fast in the gathering dusk; beyond the Sooke Hills, wispy clouds turned orange as the sun disappeared for the night.

William and I listened to speeches from a Japanese lady and a man wearing a white beret. Then a street person emerged from the darkness, wrapped in an old blanket, and disrupted the ceremony by making loud comments in a voice slurred by booze. People shifted uneasily, but nothing happened until William left my side and approached the man.

They spoke quietly, then William returned to me. The drunk said nothing more during the remaining speeches and the launching of the paper boats on the pond. Some were beautifully decorated, while others displayed only the single word *Peace* on their sails. Inside each boat, a candle burned; filled with light, the boats drifted together and then apart. Some people wept, while others closed their eyes in prayer.

After the ceremony ended, I looked at William. "That was wonderful. But what happened with that guy? You totally silenced him."

William shrugged. "I explained the importance of the ceremony. He understood."

I looked for the man, but he was gone.

William glanced at his watch. "Liz, I've got to run. I've really got to get back to work."

I was disappointed. I wondered if William was secretly a workaholic, but I didn't say anything.

He smiled with those big, green eyes. "My project must get finished, Liz. I have to deliver within days." He touched my arm. "I shouldn't have come out tonight. But I wanted to see you."

"Well, I understand. Perhaps we'll meet again?"

William nodded. "You'd better believe it."

* * *

Asleep that night, I thought I heard my cell phone ring. "William's calling," I mumbled to myself, stumbling around the room in search of the phone.

But the call was only a dream—I realized the phone had never rung. "Oh, William," I whispered, wandering to the window to gaze at the moon. "Are you thinking of me?"

In the morning I was anxious to tell Tiffany about William, but she'd gone downtown with the maid of honour. "Wedding errands," Pepper explained, as we ate breakfast together. "Tiff gave you the day off."

I yawned, still sleepy. "Maybe I'll phone William for a chat."

"Who's he?"

"This guy I met. Pepper, he's so cool. I hope you'll meet him."

"Feel like going to the park?" Pepper asked. "I'm taking Amanda to visit the Children's Zoo and see the ducks."

"Let's do it," I replied. "It's fun being with you."

I phoned William, but got his machine. *Please leave a message*, his recorded voice requested pleasantly, but I didn't. I knew I shouldn't be bothering William while he worked on his project.

The day was rainy, so the park was almost empty and virtually silent, except for the distant sound of slow-moving traffic. Above us, an eagle soared past. I wandered the pathways with Pepper, who had rain-proofed Amanda in her stroller. The flower beds were beautifully planted with many wonderful flowers. Many trees were *huge*.

"Emily Carr loved this place," Pepper said.

"Look." I pointed up at a huge nest. "There's a heron."

We watched the heron spread an enormous wing for a careful cleaning, then it lifted off from the nest. After a couple of flaps, the heron sailed gracefully down across a small lake to land near an elderly man who was feeding ducks from his park bench.

"Let's get closer," Pepper suggested.

Near a path beside the lake, we took shelter under a weeping willow. "This is more mist than rain," I whispered, watching it collect on leaves to form chubby raindrops that plopped to the ground.

We watched the man tossing birdseed to the noisy ducks crowded all around. His wooden cane was hooked over the park bench. My heart melted at the sweetness of the scene—until the man produced a package of cigarettes and lit up!

Shaking my head, I walked away with Pepper and Amanda. At Fountain Lake we stopped to watch ducks paddling in search of food amongst a carpet of lily pads. The petals of their flowers were pure white; each encircled at its heart a burst of yellow, as though the sun lived there.

"Even on a cloudy day," Pepper said, "that glow can warm your soul."

I watched a white-haired lady pass by, chatting happily with a younger man. Then I smiled fondly at Amanda, who was fascinated by the ducks. "Isn't it difficult, coping with a child? I mean, you're so young."

"Well, the servants help a lot."

"Any regrets?"

Pepper shook her head. "Amanda was born on February 14, and she'll always be my favourite Valentine. But I tell you, Liz, getting dates is tough. Lots of guys don't want a kid around."

At that moment the sun broke through the clouds, and as the day became warmer, steam began rising from the pathways. Drawn by the sound of music, we came upon an outdoor bandstand. A pretty woman with long hair was on the stage with her band, entertaining an appreciative audience seated on benches. *Music for the Trees,* read a banner behind the band. *Send a message of love to B.C.'s trees*.

We stopped to listen. Pepper and I were both impressed by the singer; I loved the idea of music serenading the trees.

"Maybe I could sign her to a contract," Pepper said. "You know, when I'm a music producer. It won't be long now."

After the concert we walked to the Inner Harbour, where Cambridge was waiting with the Daimler outside the Empress. Pepper got into the limo with Amanda, but I decided against returning to Thirteen Oaks. "You see that boat with the big sign?" I said to Pepper. "They offer a three-hour sail. I think I'll get a ticket. What a perfect day for riding the ocean waves."

We said goodbye, then I crossed Government to the Inner Harbour. There was a nice hum of activity, what with the boaters and buskers and lots of tourists. A nice-looking guy approached, smiling. It was Fossilized Pete, who'd taken us to the West Bay Marina.

"How'd that turn out?" Pete asked, after we'd exchanged hellos.

"We found the *Outlaw*."

Pete looked surprised. "Tell me more."

I decided not to mention Jason by name, but did describe his boat escaping into the night. I also told Pete about the drunk. When I finished my story, Pete smiled. "You know Laura Singlehurst, eh? She's a friend of mine. I saw Laura the other night—she was looking for someone named Pepper. She mentioned you."

We chatted for a few minutes, and then I said goodbye to Pete and climbed on board the boat. It was the *Thayne*, a 17-metre gaff-rigged ketch (as the captain told me). About a dozen tourists waited on the deck, and I said hello while searching for somewhere to sit. From below came the smell of fuel; a dinghy with an outboard was attached to the stern.

The captain was young and friendly. "We'll use the sails, once we've left port. This schooner was hand-built from bits of old Victoria houses, so it's got some nice vibes."

As we left port, I waved at people in a harbour ferry, then turned my face to the sun. As always, the water was heavy with vessels; on shore, people watched our passage from an oceanside pathway. I saw joggers and cyclists passing before some large buildings.

"Those are condos and townhouses," our captain explained to me. "It's a nice location, but the seaplanes can get noisy."

"Be careful your captain's cap doesn't blow off," I warned him, as the wind gusted briefly.

"Huh?"

"If your hat blows overboard, you're marked for drowning."

He grinned. "Hey, you're superstitious. Just like my wife."

We glided past a Coast Guard station, then a gigantic cruise ship moored at a wharf where a really big mural welcomed people to Victoria. "Cruise ships visit here every summer," our captain said. "This is a favourite stop on their journey to Alaska."

"I'd love to get on board." I felt smaller than an ant, staring up at the balconies on the many decks.

Out on the open sea, large orange sails were unfurled. Finding them, the breezes sent our vessel running swiftly forward. It was so quiet, with just the wind in our ears. One passenger felt seasick, but our captain told him to keep watching the horizon, and that seemed to help.

"Look," someone cried, pointing to starboard. "There's an orca, right beside us."

What a thrilling sight. For several minutes the whale swam near us, its dorsal fin, white "flash" and immense black body glistening each time it emerged from beneath the surface. "Sometimes this happens once we've turned off the engine," the captain told us. "There's no noise to frighten the orcas, and people say they're naturally friendly."

The captain watched me take some more photos of the beautiful whale. "Are you using colour film?"

"Sure."

"But why?" He grinned. "The orca's in black and white."

I chuckled at his joke. "Okay to use your binoculars?" I asked.

He passed me powerful Zeiss-Ikons. I trained them

on the distant Victoria shoreline, hoping to spot the *Outlaw* prowling along. I needed a break in the case, something to help crack it wide open. But luck wasn't with me.

The mysterious craft was nowhere to be seen.

* * *

On Monday I went downtown by bus. The sun was hot but the air was pleasantly free of humidity as I walked to the Cyber Station.

Inside its cool depths, I asked to use a computer terminal. There was something about Paris that had been niggling at me. I could have used a computer at Thirteen Oaks, but I needed to work away from prying eyes.

Lots of people sat at the terminals; some were tourists, speaking together in foreign languages as they read e-mail messages or surfed the Net. I read the news from my family and friends, answered everyone, then checked the Tourism Victoria Website for the name Sandown. Sure enough I found something, and soon had tracked down the truth about Bigoted Earl.

* * *

I was feeling pleased with myself as I rode beside Tiffany in the Jeep. We were heading out of Victoria on West Saanich Road, which wandered amid thick stands of trees and past scenic homes and small farms. Our destination was known only to me.

Tiffany glanced my way. "You're certain this mystery trip is necessary, Liz? I'm very busy, you know."

"Yes, yes, I do know. But you're going to see something important. Just follow my directions."

Eventually we approached a parking lot filled with vehicles. Beyond them, a large wooden grandstand rose into the air. We could hear loud cries from the spectators.

"What's this place?" Tiff asked.

"Sandown," I replied triumphantly. "It's a track. Horses race here. One's called Bigoted Earl, and it's running today." Before Tiffany could respond, I punched numbers into my cell phone. When a man answered, I gave him a short message.

"Now let's see what happens," I said to Tiffany. "This should be good."

* * *

A few minutes later, Paris came out of the grandstand. I waved at him, and he hurried forward. Then he saw Tiffany, and his face turned pale.

"Tiffany, why are you here? Liz told me there was an emergency, but she never mentioned your name."

Tiffany's blue eyes stared at Paris; she seemed confused and frightened.

He scowled at me. "I knew you'd betray me to Tiff."

"Well," I said briskly, "why not confess? You've been gambling money at Sandown Raceway. Today you're betting on Bigoted Earl, right?"

Tiffany was totally shocked. "Well, Paris?"

"I guess . . . I guess it's true."

I waited for Tiffany to throw her engagement ring at

his feet. Instead, she did nothing—absolutely nothing.

Then Paris said, "Listen, Tiff, how about a loan? I've got inside information on the race. Bigoted Earl can't fail. Let's win this one together."

I was shocked and appalled. Then, to my horror, Tiffany nodded her agreement. "Okay, I guess. But only this time, all right?"

Paris grinned. "You bet. Thanks, sweetheart."

Tiffany handed Paris a bunch of cash. As she did, my heart almost broke. What did the future hold for a girl as sweet and trusting as Tiff?

* * *

As I feared, Bigoted Earl ran out of the money. The horse was a loser, just like Paris. He stayed for more races, but we left the raceway.

"Tiffany," I pleaded, as we walked to the Jeep, "don't lend him more money. He'll just gamble it away."

"Paris needs me, Liz."

"He needs your bank account!"

"Since his father's death, I've been his constant strength."

Once again, I gave up. At Thirteen Oaks we collected Pepper, then headed to the Artful Needle for a dress fitting. After that we continued downtown for more errands. Tiff parked the Jeep at the Eaton Centre, a large mall with a British theme, and we wandered along tourist-thronged Government Street. Then I glanced east and saw that people had gathered at a nearby street.

We hurried to join the crowd. "What's going on?" Tiff asked a bicycle cop who was on traffic duty. "Is this the marathon for charity? I read about it in the newspaper."

She nodded. "A run across Canada is ending today in Victoria. The guy will pass here in a few minutes, heading for Mile Zero at the ocean."

"What charity is the runner supporting?" Pepper asked.

"This guy wants to help abused kids," the officer replied. "He was assaulted himself—by his coach when he played junior hockey. He kept the secret all through his years as an NHL player, but eventually he told and the coach went to prison."

"Telling takes such courage," Tiffany said. "It's so cool that he turned his problem into a way to help others. I like kids—I wish I could help."

She got her chance when we put donations into a can carried by a volunteer. All around us, people were cheering as the runner approached. He was young and handsome, and tears were streaming from his eyes. I started to cry, and so did the others, as everyone applauded the runner and shouted praise.

Then he was gone, trailed by TV cameras and media photographers and kids on bikes. Returning to Government Street, Tiffany talked nonstop about the runner's accomplishments. "Imagine telling on your coach. They're such authority figures, right? I mean, where'd he find the courage?"

"By taking one step at a time," Pepper replied.

7

Tiff dropped me in the Cook Street Village. I'd looked up William's address in the phone book, and decided to walk past. Just in case he was around—you know? But also because I was curious to see his home.

Thick, beautiful chestnut trees sheltered Cook Street. There was a fish and chips shop, a stationer, some food stores, and several of those ubiquitous West Coast coffee shops. I noticed a small low-rider truck pass by, throbbing with music; the driver was hidden behind tinted windows. The truck carried Washington plates.

I remembered William accepting money from someone in a similar truck, perhaps even this one. I wondered who the driver was.

Soon after, I reached William's address. He lived

near the park in a three-storey house divided into apartments. Big steps led to the building's front door. William sat on the steps.

He looked exhausted. As I approached, he hardly seemed to recognize me. Then William folded a thick envelope and stuck it away in his jeans pocket. "Hi, Liz," he said, managing a smile. "I'm so beat. I've been working around the clock."

"You got paid?"

"Yeah. Now I can send Mom to Arizona. I tell you . . ."

William stopped speaking. His eyes stared past me, down to the street corner. I followed his gaze, and saw the truck with Washington plates. William watched the truck pass by, but said nothing. When it was gone, he turned to me. "Liz, I'm dead tired. See you another time, okay?"

I was disappointed but not surprised. I'm familiar with workaholics. My dad can get totally absorbed during his police investigations, and Mom's often consumed by her cases.

I said goodnight to William and went home by bus.

* * *

I was feeling sorry for myself, but a surprise invitation soon cheered me up. Laura Singlehurst had phoned Thirteen Oaks, wanting everyone to join her at Butchart Gardens for an evening picnic.

"She especially asked for you, Liz," Pepper said, as we got ready. "There are fireworks tonight. It gets chilly after dark, so bring something warm to wear."

"Why the invitation?" I asked. "What's the occasion?"

Pepper grinned. "Who knows? Who cares?"

Tiffany stayed home with tummy problems. The rest of us piled into the Daimler; with Cambridge at the wheel, we drove north out of Victoria to Butchart Gardens.

Laura met us at the entrance. We all thanked her for the surprise, and she smiled happily. "Have you ever visited Butchart Gardens?" she asked me.

I shook my head.

"For flower lovers," Laura said, "this place is heaven on earth. There are thousands and thousands of blossoms, and they're so fragrant."

"Still nothing heard about the ransom?" Paris asked Laura.

"Not a word. The kid has gone silent. We still don't know exactly what he wants."

"I'm getting nervous," Paris said. "Maybe I should inform the police. I simply can't lose the Emily Carr— Dad treasured it."

"You're a bit late calling 911," I commented disapprovingly. "The painting could be anywhere by now— some crooked collector may have bought it."

Paris glared at me but said nothing. He was in a sulky mood, and I wished he'd stayed home.

Hart knew a lot about Butchart Gardens. "They were created by a remarkable woman named Jennie Butchart," he explained. "She loved adventures, like horseback riding and hot-air ballooning, but mostly she loved her gardens."

Hart pointed at an attractive, old-fashioned house surrounded by flowers. "Long ago, the family lived in that house. All around was the Butchart quarry, where limestone was dug to make cement."

He turned to a nearby vista of flowering plants, shrubs, and evergreens. "Jennie Butchart didn't like her view of the cement works. She planted gardens and trees to hide it, then she filled the abandoned quarries with gardens. She had a great talent for design. Pretty soon she was famous, and everyone came visiting."

Hart smiled. "In 1915 Jennie Butchart served 15,000 cups of tea to visitors. Her gardens became more and more popular, and now there's got to be easily a million visitors every year. It's beautiful here at Christmas, with the lights sparkling everywhere, but personally I love the summertime fireworks concerts. There's one tonight—they are amazing events."

"Concerts?" I said. "You mean, like a band has a concert?"

"Kind of," Hart replied. "We'll be watching fireworks set to music."

Cambridge returned from the gardens' dining room, carrying a picnic basket full of gourmet goodies Laura had ordered especially for the occasion. "We'll be eating soon," Laura promised us.

We posed for a picture with the picnic basket beside a giant boar fashioned from bronze. "Why's his nose so shiny?" I asked.

"People touch the statue for good luck," Laura explained.

"I could use some good luck," Pepper muttered, vigorously rubbing the boar's nose.

The comment caused Laura to glance at Pepper, but she said nothing.

A path beneath cedars and Douglas firs led to a lookout above the Sunken Garden. We leaned over a railing, amazed at the visual splendour spread out below. "This was a quarry," Hart explained. "Limestone from here was used to make cement. See the tall chimney in the distance? It's all that remains of the cement factory. The ivy on the quarry walls was part of Jennie Butchart's vision."

Laura looked at us. "My aunt says that Jennie used to be lowered by rope into the quarry with seeds and tools, then she spent the day creating her gardens."

"Look at that enormous dahlia," I exclaimed. "It's like a soccer ball—it's colossal."

"Wait till you see the Rose Garden," Hart said. "The West Coast has a perfect climate for growing roses. They love it here."

We watched the dancing waters of a pretty fountain located deep within the walls of the former quarry. Then we followed a pathway to grassy lawns where a large crowd was gathering for the fireworks.

"There's got to be three thousand people here," I exclaimed, with a whistle of astonishment. "Are the fireworks that good?"

Hart smiled. "Wait and see. They start at dusk."

Finding our way through the crowd, we located some open grass and spread out blankets. We were totally surrounded by beautiful flowers and many vibrant shades of green. It was a festive scene. I noticed flash cameras popping all over the crowd. People were having a good time together, their buzzing voices making them sound like a convention of gossiping locusts.

The scrumptious picnic was spread out, photographed, and drooled over. Then we dove at the food. My favourite was probably the chilled prawns with pesto mayonnaise, or maybe the teriyaki chicken, but *everything* was a fantastic taste sensation.

Since the fireworks wouldn't start until dusk, we played card games and read books. I was totally involved in a creepy tale when Pepper touched my shoulder, making me jump.

"I'm going to the snack bar, Liz. Come with me, okay?"

"Sure thing," I replied, reluctantly closing the book at an extremely suspenseful scene.

The delicate lights of Japanese lanterns shone close to the forest. The night was closing in, and I crossed my fingers for luck—a frequent habit of mine. We found our way through the chattering crowds, and then, at the snack bar, I got a surprise. A young guy behind the counter said, "You're Liz Austen, right?"

"Sure, but how'd you know?"

"Somebody left an envelope for you, and described your looks. They were right—you're gorgeous."

"Out of three thousand people," I said doubtfully, "you recognized me?"

"Well . . ."

"Come on, Liz," Pepper said impatiently. "Take the envelope, and let's get going. Otherwise we'll miss the fireworks."

"Okay," I replied.

My name was on the envelope; inside was a brief message written in emerald ink. *Liz*, it said, *Meet me at the Japanese Garden at exactly 10 tonight. Please don't be late. Don't tell anyone—this is very important.*

The message was signed with a single letter. My

heart skipped a beat when I saw it. It was a W—as in William.

* * *

As we returned to the others, slowly finding our way past the many blankets and lawn chairs, I glanced at Pepper. "You gave that guy at the snack bar a big tip. I guess you liked him."

She shrugged. "He was okay."

Pepper didn't ask about my message, and I didn't volunteer any information. I was confused by what it said, and needed time to think.

Our blankets were on a slope, facing a small lake. Beyond the water, the forest was silhouetted against a pale orange sky. Looking up, I searched for stars. Then I smiled at Laura. "Thanks for treating us all to Butchart Gardens. I'll never forget this—it's so lovely here."

"You're very welcome, Liz."

A starburst lit the pale sky. Thousands of voices went *oooooooh*, then everyone cheered as shooting stars exploded above—purple, white, blue, green, red, everything!

From the trees came beautiful music—violins, and the voice of a singer. More fireworks shot above us, then displays suddenly ignited. Multicoloured fountains arose at the lake, twirling sparkles into the night, while a huge golden hive came to life with artificial bees twirling noisily in the night air. Beyond the lake, a colourful train choo-chooed past, as cameras flashed from the crowd. Amazingly, everything was made of fireworks.

"How have they done this?" I exclaimed. "It's magical."

I looked at my watch. Almost 10 o'clock—time to go! "I'll be back soon," I said to Laura. "I've got someone to meet."

She looked surprised. "What's going on?"

I shrugged, trying to appear nonchalant. "I'm, um, meeting someone. I won't be long."

"I'm not so sure . . ."

"Please, Laura. This is important."

"Well, okay, but take my cell phone." Laura handed me a tiny ruby-coloured phone. Then she turned to Paris. "Got your cell here?"

"Yes," he replied.

"If you need us," Laura told me, "push Memory-1 on my cell. Paris will answer."

"Where should we meet?" I asked.

"At the parking lot, following the fireworks. You remember where the Daimler is parked?"

I nodded.

"We'll see you there."

Slowly I found a path through the throng while *oooooohs* and *ahhhhhhhs* sounded from open mouths, cameras flashed, and deep *booms* echoed from the hills. Leaving the show behind, I was soon alone in the vast central gardens. I looked up at the fireworks and saw whirling colours and fireballs trailing diamonds in their wake, and even a comet burning across the sky.

"Totally cool," I whispered to myself.

The evening smelled of summer; all around, flowers slumbered in their beds. As I followed signposts along a cinder pathway, I discovered places where invisible pools of warm air had gathered, filled with sweet fragrances. Half expecting to meet the ghost of Jennie Butchart wandering her earthly paradise, I finally reached the Japanese Garden. Lights shone on delicate plants, and water trickled between ponds where small statues represented pagodas.

Where was William? I felt very alone, and was glad that Laura had provided her cell phone. Was this some kind of hoax? As I hesitated, wondering what to do, I heard my name.

Liz, a voice called from the trees. *Liz! Liz!*

* * *

I squinted, looking for movement. Light flashed—once, twice, three times. I was confused for a moment, then realized I was looking at reflectors on the heels of someone's joggers.

Someone who was running down a path, away from me.

I quickly followed. The path sloped down, following a zigzag pattern lower and lower through the trees. I became aware of the ocean's salty smell, and I could hear waves slapping against the shore.

The roar of an engine split the night. I was startled by the noise, but pressed on. Moments later, I reached the ocean. The path ended at a wooden dock. Out on the water I saw a boat zooming away under the stars; no name was visible. At the controls was a figure, impossible to identify.

A surprise awaited me—lying on the dock was a metal tube. "Wait a minute," I exclaimed to myself.

"The thief at Thirteen Oaks put *Klee Wyck* inside a tube just like this."

I opened the tube at one end. Something was in there. Working quickly, I soon was able to remove a painting and unroll it. To my utter astonishment, I found myself gazing at a picture of a woman with a laughing face.

"Wow," I exclaimed. "This is the missing painting! This is *Klee Wyck*."

* * *

Seconds later I punched Memory-1 on the cell phone. When Paris answered, I immediately asked for Laura. "Guess what?" I exclaimed, and quickly told the news.

"We'll be right there," Laura said. "Guard that painting."

I heard Paris yelp, "What painting?" followed by dead air. Switching off the phone, I contemplated the laughing face of *Klee Wyck*. How wonderful that she'd been found!

Voices soon approached through the trees, then I saw Hart and the others. Pushing Laura aside, Paris hurried forward to grab the painting from my hands. "Amazing," he exclaimed. "This is marvellous. *Klee Wyck* has actually been returned."

"But why give back the painting?" Laura demanded. "It doesn't make sense."

"I guess that kid got cold feet and decided to abandon the thing." Paris kissed the painting. "I'm so happy. This ranks with the time I hit the jackpot at Vegas. No—it's even better."

Laura turned to me. "Liz, what happened?"

They listened to my story, then Laura smiled. "You deserve a reward. Don't you agree, Paris?"

"I guess you're right, Laura. Liz did find the painting."

"But why me?" I said. "Why the voice calling my name, and why the message in the envelope? What's going on? Nothing makes sense."

"Who cares," Paris exclaimed happily. "I've got my painting back. That's what matters."

Hart looked at him. "It's *our* painting, Paris. It belongs to the family."

"Okay, sure." Paris looked around at us. "Remember, you're sworn to secrecy. Keep a tight lid on this, okay?"

* * *

On Tuesday evening, Paris summoned a family gathering in the library at Thirteen Oaks. He wanted everyone to see the *Klee Wyck*, safely returned to its place above the fireplace.

Laura Singlehurst was there, looking glorious in a spectacular fashion creation. Major Wright also attended, which was a surprise. Somehow he'd learned the truth about the brief disappearance of *Klee Wyck*.

I stood beside Tiff, admiring Emily Carr's painting; the totems and the longhouses were captured with such artistry. I smiled, looking at the spirited face of the Laughing One, then I snapped out of my revery when Paris began shouting at Hart.

"I told you—*no way*." I stared at Paris—a vein bulged at his temple.

"We do not involve the police. Not now, not ever."

"But things don't add up, Paris. Why steal the painting, then return it?"

"It would be hard to make money with a stolen painting," Laura suggested. "Maybe the thief gave up trying."

Paris nodded. "I agree with Laura. Jason stole the wrong thing."

"If so," Hart responded, "he'll be back, looking for the right thing. I agree with Liz—something is rotten in the state of Denmark."

"Huh?" Paris said. "What's that mean?"

"It's nothing," Hart replied disdainfully. "Forget it."

Paris laughed. "Hart, you are such a fool."

Laura looked at the deMornay brothers. "In my opinion, don't involve the police. What are your thoughts, Major Wright?"

The Major focused his attention on the family circle. "I agree with Miss Singlehurst and Paris. We can't risk informing the police. Liz Austen's got a hyperactive imagination. Everyone in Winnipeg knows that."

Tiffany turned to the Major, annoyed. "Liz and her brother are famous crime-busters, Daddy."

"Tiffany, this is not a crime. The painting is hanging on the wall, in front of our eyes. Let's stay focused— we can't let anything spoil my daughter's romantic wedding."

Glancing into the dark hallway, I saw the butler. Cambridge lurked in the shadows, listening to every word. Noticing my stare, however, he hastily entered the library with refreshments on a wheeled trolley.

* * *

The gathering broke up soon afterward, with Paris ordering us to remain silent about anything involving Emily Carr's unknown masterpiece.

"Let's keep this in the family," he said, repeating one of his favourite arguments.

Later that evening, Tiff and I were still in the library. The security lasers were off; Hart had promised to return later to enter the code. (After the theft Paris had changed the code from 7-7-6-6, a classic example of closing the barn door too late.) Hart and the others had scattered to distant corners of the moody old mansion, leaving us alone with *Klee Wyck*.

"It's good Emily Carr went to those villages," I said, studying the painting, "so we've got her take on British Columbia long ago. I wish I could have met her."

Tiff shivered. "I'd be scared the monkey would bite."

I wandered around the bookshelves, studying the titles. The deMornay family liked to read; recent bestsellers shared the shelves with some really old books.

"This is a history of Thirteen Oaks," I told Tiff, selecting a mouldy oldy from the shelf. "Hey, look. There's a map of the estate in here. Maybe we could learn something."

I settled down on a leather sofa to read. But moments later, Pepper rushed into the library. "Liz, Tiff. Put down that book and come quickly!"

Tossing it down, I jumped to my feet. The three of us hurried into the dark hallway.

"I've looked everywhere for you," Pepper said. "There's been a message from that guy Jason. From the *Outlaw*."

"That's amazing," I exclaimed.

We hurried through the old mansion. "We're going to the family office," Pepper explained. "Jason said to wait at the office, and he'd call back. It's you he's calling, Liz."

* * *

A long time passed while I paced back and forth in the office. I kept thinking about Jason's call—what could it mean?

"I'll make some lemonade," Pepper eventually offered, leaving for the kitchen.

When she returned, we glugged down the delicious, cold beverage. Then I stood up. "Forget Jason—he was pulling a hoax. It's time for bed."

"Are you sure?" Pepper asked.

"Yes—I'm sick of this. I'm going to the library to get that history of the estate. I need some bedtime reading."

The laser beams were still down at the library. I was looking forward to reading about Thirteen Oaks, but instead I got a surprise.

The book was gone.

8

I searched the library, but found nothing. The next day I returned with Pepper, and we both tried, again without success.

"This is so weird," I said, as we sat with glasses of lemonade. "First the painting disappears, and now a book. What gives?"

Pepper shook her head. "It beats me."

Later, driving downtown in the Jeep, I debated telling Tiffany about the Curious Incident of the Book in the Night. Only three days remained until her wedding, and Tiff was sometimes very agitated. Finally I decided against mentioning the book. Tiff looked tense, and I didn't want anything else to bother her.

We met Paris downtown at Ming's for a delicious Chinese meal with friends of theirs. I was the fifth wheel, but I didn't mind—I liked the other couple and, anyway, William had called, and I'd be seeing him later that evening. Nothing could bother me.

I have to admit that Paris was good for Tiff when she was moody. He whispered sweet nothings in her ear, and soon she was cheerful again. Leaving them at the table, I went to the washroom with their friend, Jennifer Scriver.

"Have you known Paris long?" I asked, as we combed our hair in front of the mirror.

Jennifer nodded. "I went to Shawnigan Lake School, same as Paris and Tiffany. He was a fun guy, but something's gone wrong."

"Meaning what?"

Jennifer looked at me in the mirror. "Paris went from grief about his dad to reckless behaviour. Now he's unstable, and looking for security. Someone to cling to."

"And Tiff is rock solid."

"You bet," Jennifer said. "Tiffany knows exactly what she wants—marriage and a family. She's also got a bank account. For Paris, it's the perfect package."

* * *

As we left the restaurant, Paris took Tiffany aside. I could see her shaking her head, then finally she frowned and handed him some money. Paris waved goodbye to me, and walked away with the other couple.

"They're heading for Sandown Raceway," Tiff said glumly. "I refused to go."

"I'm visiting William," I said. "Come with me. You need cheering up."

"You're sure William won't mind?"

"I doubt it."

I was right—William welcomed us warmly. His funky place was filled with objects and art that hinted at a unique personality. As I roamed the walls, studying everything, Tiff and William chatted in the tiny kitchen.

Heading downstairs, we met William's neighbour in the lobby; Sadie was the singer who'd been at the park, performing a concert for the trees. We enjoyed a friendly chat with her, then went outside.

"Sadie's multi-talented," William told us. "She paints miniatures—very beautiful. You should see the flowers with their tiny petals. Victoria is full of incredible artists."

Behind the house was a garage that William had converted into a studio. Inside, we saw his landscapes—he really loved British Columbia's forests, mountains and oceans. William concentrated on big vistas and filled his scenes with light.

"I love your art," I said. "It's so like Emily Carr."

"I certainly admire her work," William said, "and her courage. She didn't do things the easy way. She got into her canoe, and went out into nature. She went in pursuit of truth—to show the totems in their natural setting, in the forest and the villages, how they really looked. Emily Carr went through tremendous difficulties in pursuit of her art—you can imagine the social pressures against her. That's so admirable for a woman of her time, being brave enough to chase such a beautiful dream."

"I love listening to you," I said.

"That's good, Liz, because—"

A shrill *brrring* shattered the moment. I looked in annoyance at the phone, a paint-smeared relic with a rotary dial.

William picked it up and said, "William speaking."

Frowning, he listened to the caller. "You can have it back," he said angrily. "It's dirty."

Then William stared at the phone. "He hung up."

"Who was it?" I asked.

"No one important," William replied, avoiding my eyes. "Listen, I need a sweater. Wait here, okay? I'll get one from my apartment in the big house."

Tiff and I wandered around the studio, looking at canvases stacked against the walls. Then I stopped at a wooden desk in the corner; scattered across it were some photos, face down.

"I wonder what these are?" I reached toward the nearest photo. "Maybe preliminary studies for William's next project."

Then I heard William's voice. "Don't touch those."

Startled, I turned toward the sound. William stood in the doorway, pointing at me. "Liz, please don't touch those pictures."

"Sure," I replied, raising my hands. "No problem."

William scooped up the photos, dropped them into a drawer, and turned the key. "It's just," he said, pocketing the key, "that I'm . . . very superstitious."

"Me, too," I replied.

"Letting anyone see my next project would be really bad luck. You understand, Liz?"

"Of course." I studied William's handsome face.

His eyes flicked from me to the desk, then back to me.

Was I making a mistake here?

"My uncle works on the pilot boat," William told us. "It's going out tonight and he's invited us along. Care to go?"

We both happily agreed.

"What's a pilot boat?" I asked later from the Jeep's back seat, as Tiff reached Cook Street.

William turned to her. "Let's stop at the Chateau Victoria, and I'll explain."

At the upscale hotel we took an elevator to the 18th floor, where seagulls winged past large windows enclosing a restaurant high above the city streets. It was early evening, and the descending sun made every colour intense. Beyond an assortment of roofs, we saw the green trees of Beacon Hill Park and a big freighter on the beautiful waters of the ocean strait. Visible beneath the mountains on the strait's far side was the city of Port Angeles, Washington.

"Lots of oceangoing vessels pass along this strait," William said. "In these narrow waters they need a nautical pilot on the ship to guide the captain safely through. The pilot is taken out to the vessel from Victoria on board the pilot boat. Uncle Joe is the boat's captain. We're going out as his guests."

"Cool," Tiffany exclaimed. "I need a distraction from all the wedding talk."

"Thanks so much," I said, smiling at William. This time I thought to myself, *He's so nice.*

* * *

Soon we reached Ogden Point, home to the pilot boat. The small vessel was sheltered from storms by a large breakwater, where people strolled as darkness arrived. Scuba divers explored the waters near the breakwater; some had neon glow ropes, which looked eerie shining beneath the surface. Nearby were large wharves; at one was a U.S. navy vessel, in town for a visit.

On board the pilot boat we were introduced to its captain, William's friendly uncle Joe. "A cruise ship named the *Galaxy* is passing by tonight," he explained, "bound for Alaska. We're taking a pilot to board the *Galaxy*, out on the strait."

"Why doesn't it stop in Victoria and collect the pilot before it sails?"

"Not all cruise ships visit here. Some passengers prefer a bigger city like Vancouver, but others find our town very friendly. Some locals even dress up in old-fashioned garb and hand out flowers at the cruise ship wharf. The passengers love that."

"Is your work dangerous?" I asked.

"It can be, especially in a storm. Our boat is mighty small alongside some of those cruise ships."

The pilot boat was indeed small, with an open deck and an enclosed cabin where the pilot was working on some papers. As Uncle Joe started the engine, he pointed at a blue heron standing near the shore. It looked so regal, totally focused on the water as it hungrily awaited a passing meal. "We call that heron Doug," Uncle Joe explained. "Doug's lived in this basin for 23 years."

Reaching open waters, Uncle Joe opened the throttle. A powerful roar sounded from below decks as the boat gathered speed, leaving a plume of spray in its wake. The boat had a solid hull and lots of power, so it moved smoothly through the waves.

Wearing fluorescent life preservers, we stood beside William's uncle on the deck. He was at the wheel, controlling the boat with an effortless grace. Behind us, the lights of Victoria glowed along the shoreline. It was a warm night; stars lit the dark sky as surf rushed away across the restless depths.

I pointed at the Dallas Road cliffs. "I guess that's Beacon Hill Park, up on top. What's the other dark area, farther down Dallas Road? Is that Ross Bay Cemetery, where Emily Carr is buried?"

"Yup," William replied.

"Maybe I'll go visit her grave."

I asked Uncle Joe if he'd seen the *Outlaw*. "The name sounds familiar," he said, looking at my drawing of the mystery boat. He promised to watch for it, then answered more questions about his work. "The worst thing is the fog," he told us. "You can imagine—buried in swirling mists while you're rocking and rolling on heavy seas, trying to park this small craft beside a huge elephant like the *Galaxy*. That can get pretty hair-raising."

"Ever had a man overboard?" William asked.

He nodded. "Pilots have to jump between vessels— sometimes one lands in the drink. But we're quick to save them. We have a safety procedure which we practise frequently."

The cruise ship approached out of the night, glittering with lights. It looked like a birthday cake with every candle glowing, and it was soooo big. My heart pounded with excitement; this was an amazing experience.

We moved in close to the *Galaxy*. It was impossible to see the upper decks, so far above; down at the water level, a large open door awaited the pilot. He wore a shirt and tie, plus a corduroy jacket and tan trousers. As we moved in on the cruise ship, the pilot tensed, ready to leap across the cold waters.

"Now," William exclaimed, as the vessels met. Immediately the pilot sailed through the air, landing nimbly inside the cruise ship. We three cheered and applauded; the grinning pilot bowed deeply, as Uncle Joe powered our vessel away from the *Galaxy*.

"Gosh," I said dreamily, watching the cruise ship's radiant lights twinkle away into the night. "That is such a vision."

* * *

The next morning I awoke long before dawn. Unable to sleep, I went to the kitchen. Cambridge was already there, moodily preparing coffee. Outside the window, birdsong heralded the coming day. "They're up early," I commented, glancing into the garden. "What a sweet sound they make."

A grunt was the butler's only reply. I pressed on, determined to remain cheerful. "Do local buses run this early?"

He glanced at the clock. "Yes, Miss Austen."

"How would I catch a bus to Dallas Road? I'm thinking of walking the cliffs, then visiting Emily Carr's grave."

The butler's shaggy eyebrows rose. "Why Emily Carr?"

I shrugged. "I'm a fan."

Cambridge disappeared from the room, then returned with a well-thumbed paperback. "This is the John Adams guide to Ross Bay Cemetery," he told me. "Take it with you—there are lots of fascinating stories about the people in that cemetery. It dates back to 1873, so you'll find the graves of many famous types. The quirky ones usually have the best stories. Like Emily Carr, for example."

"Thanks, Cambridge. You're very kind."

"It's no problem," he replied. "You see—"

Cambridge was interrupted by a plaintive *meow*. Opening the outside door, he looked down at a scrawny cat with ragged fur. "This stray's been coming by for food," Cambridge said, preparing a dish of leftovers, as the waif rubbed around his ankles, purring. "My brother owns a pet store in the Fairfield Plaza. He's always pleading with people—don't give pets as Christmas presents, because they can get abandoned once the festivities are over."

Cambridge watched the cat hungrily devour its feast. "Buy a pet in January, once you're certain it's not just a holiday whim."

What a nice man, I thought a little later, while hurrying through the quiet Uplands to the nearest bus stop. After a pleasant journey, I stepped from the bus in the quiet James Bay neighbourhood. At Dallas Road a sign pointed the way to a beach named for marathon runner Steve Fonyo. I photographed the sign, then moved on.

A paved walkway wandered along the clifftop, with the occasional path or stairs providing access to the ocean far below. In the pale sky, swallows flitted past, appearing to play, but probably chasing McInsects for breakfast. Over at the western hills the newborn sun reflected from the windows of homes, transforming the glass into sparkling jewels.

I wandered along the pathway, pausing to watch the pilot boat heading toward a large freighter. The tide was out, exposing wet seaweed on the rocks below; in the distance were the mountains, pale blue under the pink sky of early morning.

The path led to Beacon Hill Park, where a large sign announced this as Mile Zero of the Trans-Canada Highway. Inside the park, thick bushes and trees grew along the pathway. I studied a tugboat on the water; it looked motionless, straining against the mighty weight of the logs it towed. I watched birds winging across the water on important business, and heard pleasant whistling cries from within the trees. Yellow broom was scattered everywhere, lending its sweet fragrance to the morning air.

I then spotted the world's tallest totem pole, which I remembered from researching Victoria on the Net. Nearby was the hill that probably gave this park its name; in the days before lighthouses, a beacon up there would have warned boats away from the cliffs.

Before long I left Beacon Hill Park behind, but continued walking above the cliff. The early morning sun was on the ocean, shining a golden path for my pleasure. Beside me was a large green space, then a road and some small houses. White and purple wildflowers scattered their colours along the cliff. A kayaker was out, enjoying the good life, B.C. style. Seagulls called across the water, and waves lapped softly against the rocky beaches below. A blue heron lifted away from the water, circled, and was slowly airborne on impressive wings.

Finally I reached Ross Bay Cemetery, an oasis of shady trees beside the blue ocean. I opened my packsack, looking for water and more film, then leaned against a marble tombstone while I flipped through the cemetery guidebook. It was loaded with interesting stories.

At Emily Carr's grave, I was touched by the inscription, *Artist and author, lover of nature*. I took a photo, then wandered on. I stayed on the paved walkways, wanting to avoid crossing an unmarked grave (as many people know, doing so can cause your body to develop a serious rash). I studied a holly tree and then a monkey puzzle tree, its curved branches so like the tails of playful monkeys. One tombstone was called Pooley's marble angel; it was said to cry on nights with a full moon, according to the guidebook.

"I should check this out with William," I murmured to myself. "Too bad we missed the full moon."

In the guidebook, Cambridge had underlined several notes in green ink. Walking west, I studied the notes, trying to find a pattern. One note referred to a teenager who'd drowned in the Gorge waterway, so perhaps Cambridge—

Somewhere in the cemetery, a stick cracked loudly. I lifted my head and looked around—there were a lot of big tombstones. Bushes and trees also provided hiding places.

I could feel my heart thumping. For moments I

waited. Nothing stirred but the occasional leaf drifting to earth.

I stared at a cobweb, shining on a stone cross—it was beautiful, but I felt frightened. I decided to go home; closing the guidebook, I lowered my packsack to stuff the book away. But my camera accidentally fell, smacking hard against the paved walkway. Annoyed, I picked up the camera—had it been damaged?

He came out of nowhere, a blur of motion.

Energy pumped through my body. I rolled swiftly aside to avoid the attack, then sprang into the ready position I knew from martial arts. Behind me, a hill fell down to Dallas Road. I breathed deeply, centring my energy and power in my torso.

The attacker wore a ski mask—all I could see were his eyes. For a moment he stared, then he lunged at me. Stepping swiftly aside and bringing up my foot, I kicked out at his leg. He yelled in pain and surprise, then went over the side. As he disappeared, I heard branches breaking and rocks pouring down the slope.

Running to the edge, I looked down. The guy stood up, painfully and slowly, and gave me a malignant stare before limping quickly away. Then he was gone from sight.

I knew what I had to do. I was going straight to the police.

9

I called Laura from a pay phone at the nearby Fairfield Plaza. She answered on the first ring and promised to join me ASAP. While waiting for Laura, I kept an eye on Fairfield Road; a car passed with Paris at the wheel, and that surprised me. He didn't seem the early-morning type.

Nervously I paced, watching shopkeepers opening their premises for the day. They were a relaxed crowd, exchanging greetings in the sunshine as they got ready, and I felt slightly better.

I saw Laura's BMW pull into the lot. As she stepped from the car, tall and elegant and so in control, I ran quickly to her. I guess I needed a hug more than I'd realized.

"I was so scared," I told Laura, as we headed for police headquarters in her car.

She patted my hand. "I know how you feel, Liz. I went through a similar experience."

After parking, we walked to the ultramodern police station on Caledonia Street. A detective took us into her office, where she poured coffee for Laura and bottled water for me. She listened carefully to all the details, then told us she'd be in touch if anything came up.

Back outside, I walked with Laura to her car. She'd offered to take me to the Inner Harbour. "I probably won't mention the attack to anyone," I said. "Tiffany would be really upset."

"That's a good idea," Laura agreed.

"Do you think this wedding makes sense?"

Laura smiled. "I've got an opinion, Liz, but I won't comment publicly."

* * *

At the Inner Harbour all kinds of people were out strolling, enjoying the musicians and artists. Boats of every type lined the wharves near the Empress Hotel, which glowed in the warmth of the sun. Some people were having their picture taken in front of the hotel, and other tourists were boarding red double-decker buses for tours of the city.

As arranged, I met Pepper at the statue of Captain Cook. We leaned against a stone wall, checking out the yachts and people below. The happy scene made me feel better. Four young men were singing "The Lion Sleeps Tonight." They harmonized without musical instruments, and received loud applause when the song ended. Everyone's mood seemed good—this was a beautiful place to be sharing.

I looked at the Empress. "Tiffany's in there right now, meeting with Major Wright. Tiff told me she's got news for her father, but she wouldn't tell me what it is."

Descending stone stairs, Pepper and I joined the crowd strolling the Lower Causeway. "I can't believe all the languages I'm hearing," I commented. "People must visit Victoria from the entire globe."

We paused to watch musicians from Peru performing on the causeway against the backdrop of the Legislative Buildings. Two men played panpipes—the music sweet and haunting—while another thumped a drum. The musicians were having fun, occasionally dancing in a circle around an open instrument case that awaited donations from onlookers.

We moved on. "I was interested in the band members' shoes," I said. "They seemed to fit each guy's personality, except for the tall one. He was heavy-set, but he wore paper-thin dancing shoes."

"You're quite the detective," Pepper said. Then she glanced at me. "How do you think the painting was stolen from Thirteen Oaks, Liz? Got any theories?"

"Someone inside the house must have been involved. Otherwise, how did the thief get past the security codes at the library?"

"Who do you think it was?"

I shook my head. "I can't say. There are too many suspects, and there's no real evidence."

As we continued our short walk, Pepper hummed a cheerful tune. A number of tents had been set up for a FolkFest, not far from the Empress. Arts and crafts were on display from all over the province. Pottery, jewellery, sweet-smelling soaps—even a First Nations raven mask with copper eyes.

A feature of the FolkFest was free entertainment on a large stage. Sitting on aluminum stands, we watched young Ukrainian dancers high-kick in bright costumes, while tiny girls from the audience joined in the fun, bouncing around in front of the stage to the rousing music, their parents watching from close by.

"I'm so lucky the servants help with Amanda," Pepper said. "Kids are so much work."

"What about her father helping?"

"He left town," Pepper replied. "You know, Liz, I can't imagine being a teenager alone with a baby, carrying diaper bags everywhere. I never realized the work involved—and the worry. I'm always freaked about Amanda—like, is she safe?"

"You mean from kidnappers?"

"I guess so," Pepper replied. "But I never thought about kidnappers before now. I just meant being safe from falling down. That kind of thing."

"Sorry," I said, feeling foolish.

"Don't worry, Liz," Pepper replied. "You're nice, and so is Tiffany. I wish she wouldn't marry Paris."

"Why?"

"For starters, he's a control freak. He's lucky that Tiffany is so sweet-natured—other women would tell Paris to take a hike." Pepper sighed. "Everything changed for Paris when our parents died. Pater's will contained a large cash payment for each kid. Hart made a smart investment with his legacy, but I lost mine buying into a dot-com company that failed."

"That's too bad."

Pepper shrugged. "Anyway, Paris totally went stupid with his legacy. My brother's lifestyle was wild—you can't imagine the parties at Thirteen Oaks. The clothes he bought—incredible. Plus crazy stunts, very expensive stuff. Like flying his friends in chartered helicopters to Whistler for snowboarding and more parties. I've seen him burn through so much, so fast."

"Does Tiffany know about this?"

Pepper nodded. "Anyway, I guess Paris blew all Pater's money. Now he's back to his allowance from the family trust. For me the allowance is plenty to live on, but Paris is a different breed of cat."

"Tiffany is so trusting," I said. "She always looks for the good side in people. Major Wright is a pretty nice guy, but basically an emotional manipulator. He's decided this marriage makes sense for Tiffany, and he thinks her doubts are just pre-wedding jitters."

"She's bought into that?"

"So far," I replied. "Tiff really loves and respects her dad. She values his opinion." Lost in thought, I absent-mindedly ran my fingers through my hair. Then I turned to Pepper. "You know what Tiff believes? If she gives Paris enough love, he'll get over his problems. And I'm just not certain it's possible."

* * *

We visited the food stands, where the goodies looked scrumptious and the smells were so delicious. I settled on a vegetarian pita from the Mediterranean stand, perogies from the Polish White Eagle Association, and

Rose's "Awesome" chocolate cake from the Jewish Community Centre.

People were eating at outdoor tables. "I'll tell you the problem with Paris," Pepper commented, as we looked for vacant chairs. "Too much money, and no Pater to control him. Our father ruled by fear, and Paris always toed the line. He wasn't a rebel until Pater died. Then my brother went crazy, doing all the things that would have scandalized Pater." She paused. "Of course, I'm not perfect, either. Pater was *so* upset when I got pregnant." Pepper shook her head. "What a crazy family I was born into, Liz, but I love them anyway. They're my kin."

"It's fun to know you, Pepper."

She smiled. "You, too."

At a sunny table we sat down next to a mother and her kids; when a ladybug landed on our table, the eldest girl said, "Now we'll all have good luck."

That superstition was new to me, and I thanked the girl for it. "We need some luck," I said, thinking of Tiffany. "I'll be watching for more ladybugs."

Pepper looked into the distance. "Wow," she murmured. "Who is this?"

Turning, I saw William walking toward our table. He was tall and so blond in the sunshine, and people noticed him. Seeing me, William's face broke into a beautiful smile.

"Liz, you're here. And you're safe."

"Sure, I'm fine," I replied, and introduced Pepper. "Why are you surprised?"

"I heard something happened at the cemetery," William said. "Is it true?"

"Yes, but how'd you find out?"

For a moment, William looked confused. "It was . . . well, from someone I know."

"Someone in the police?"

William shook his head. "No. You see—"

The ringing of my cell phone interrupted William. When I answered, I heard Tiffany's voice. "Liz," she exclaimed, "it was horrible."

Walking away from Pepper and William, I covered my ear against the noisy crowd. "Tiff, what's wrong?"

"I told Daddy I couldn't marry Paris, and he got so upset. Liz, he was crying. In the Empress, in front of everyone. People were staring."

"But . . ."

"It was just a mess, Liz. I can't hurt Daddy's feelings, ever again. I'm going ahead with the wedding."

"Tiff, where are you? I'll come to you—we'll talk."

"Not now. Daddy's so upset, he needs me. I'll stay a while with him, okay? Then I'll go home to Thirteen Oaks. I'll see you there."

"Sure, but—"

"Liz, I gotta go. Talk to you later."

The call upset me greatly, but I said nothing to William or Pepper. Leaving the FolkFest, we walked together to a transit stop where Pepper caught a bus. She was heading home to Thirteen Oaks, to see her darling Amanda. We waved goodbye, then William turned to me. "There's something I've wanted to mention. You see . . ."

Silently, I waited for him to continue.

Then William shook his head. "Maybe later, Liz." He paused, thinking. "There's a special event tonight at Carr House, which is the birthplace of Emily Carr. They're holding a Victorian salon, with refreshments and singing around the piano. Care to go with me?"

"Certainly."

William and I lingered at the Inner Harbour until evening came to the city. He seemed worried, but said nothing about his thoughts. He was very quiet as we strolled south on Government Street.

Carr House reminded me of an old-fashioned doll-house with its little windows and gingerbread decorations. In the garden, small signs carried passages from Emily Carr's writings. Reading them, William cheered up. "Emily Carr was also a prolific author," he told me. "Ever read her *Book of Small*? It describes her childhood here. When Emily was a girl, she'd come outside and sing to the family cow!"

I laughed. "It's nice to see you smile again," I told William.

At the side door we were welcomed by Jan, the cheerful woman in charge of Carr House. She knew William well because of his interest in the famous artist; after the introductions, she beamed at William. "It's about time you found someone special."

He grinned and shrugged and shuffled his feet, while Jan and I exchanged a smile.

Inside the house I met Jan's friendly daughters. She explained that the "marbled" wallpaper was hand-painted, and the elaborate outfits hanging on pegs were similar to the clothes worn by Emily and other members of the Carr family.

"People come to Victoria from all over the world," Jan told me, "just to visit the scenes of Emily Carr's life. Many are like pilgrims—they can relate to her struggles. She was an artist ahead of her time, and quite misunderstood. Much of the fame happened after her death. Do you know, only 50 people attended her funeral. Sad, eh?"

"Personally," William said, "I love this place. Imagine, Emily Carr's spirit may still linger here, within these very walls."

The parlour was exquisitely furnished in the Victorian manner. Above the fireplace was a large oval mirror supported by two fish carved from wood; I also noticed a framed portrait of the famous monkey, Woo, wearing a dress with a big yellow bow. "When Emily Carr lay dying," Jan told us, "that portrait of Woo was near her bed. She really must have loved her little friend."

Several seniors sat on velvet chairs, singing along as a lady made enthusiastic music at the piano. We joined in for "A Bicycle Built for Two," our voices loud. Then I glanced out the window. Into this perfect scene came a white horse pulling a white carriage, its big wheels slowly turning. A couple sat in the carriage, enjoying an outing through the yesteryear streets of the James Bay heritage neighbourhood.

But I got a surprise. The man in the carriage was Tiffany's father, Major Wright. Who was the woman?

* * *

Outside Carr House, William and I speculated about the woman's identity. Then I lowered my head, feeling shy. "I've got an idea."

"What's that?"

"Feel like going to the Ross Bay Cemetery?"

"Sure, but why?"

Now it was my turn to shuffle my feet. "You see, in the cemetery there's a stone angel. She's said to cry during a full moon. Maybe it's true."

William glanced up at the quarter moon. "But . . ."

"I don't really care about the angel, William. I just thought it would be a nice quiet place . . ." My voice trailed off. To be truthful, being with William had made me forget about the attack, but now I wasn't too sure about going back there.

But before I could say anything more, William nodded. "Next stop, Ross Bay Cemetery."

We walked east along Dallas Road. Above the ocean the sky glowed with stars and moonlight; we saw a ship passing by, its lights shining in the night. The tree-shaded streets of the city were quiet as people settled in; I saw a man walking two Scottie pups, but otherwise nothing stirred.

At the cemetery I paused, feeling nervous. I remembered the attack, but I overcame my fear. "Let's keep moving," I said to William. All around were the dim outlines of really old monuments to people who had once lived and loved in the homes of Victoria. Now they slumbered here; I somehow felt that their spirits accepted our presence on this beautiful night.

William looked at me. "Liz . . ."

My heart was beating in triple time. What would happen next? "William . . ."

I saw a movement in the dark trees. "Someone's there."

William laughed nervously. "You're joking, right?"

I shook my head. "I saw something."

"What are you saying—a ghost?"

"I doubt it." I looked at William. "I'm going to investigate."

"I'll go with you."

"Thanks," I said gratefully.

Out on the ocean a seabird cried, breaking the silence. Cautiously we moved through the cemetery, then finally took shelter behind a large tombstone. Close by was a monument, very wide and very tall. Carved into the marble were names and dates; at the top was a cross, and the name *deMornay*. A single red rose lay on the monument.

Standing nearby was Cambridge, the butler from Thirteen Oaks.

As we approached, Cambridge turned in surprise. "Miss Austen?" he said, wiping tears from his eyes. "Why are you here?"

"We're, um . . . out for a walk. Are you okay, sir? I mean, you've been crying."

"It's just the blues, Miss Austen. Occasionally I come here with a rose for Lady deMornay. She's the person who hired me to work at Thirteen Oaks. She was a fine, fine woman."

I nodded. "Hart and Pepper both miss her a lot. I'm not so sure how Paris feels."

Cambridge shook his head. "Master Paris just sold her painting at auction. Can you imagine? His own mother, and he sells her portrait for money."

Suddenly I slapped my forehead. "Listen, I'm being so rude. Please, let me introduce my friend."

To my pleasure, Cambridge knew William's name. "I follow the local art scene," he explained, "and people call you a rising star."

"Wow." William looked astonished. "That is so amazing."

"Your work is influenced by Emily Carr, I understand. In time you'll find your own, unique voice, but for now she's an excellent role model."

"That is just so nice," William enthused, shaking Cambridge's hand. "Thank you very much!"

I smiled, happy for William.

10

Early the next morning I talked to Tiffany, who was feeling slightly better. "It'll be a good marriage," she promised me. "Besides, I simply can't upset Daddy. What if his heart fails? Our family doctor warned me that Daddy has high blood pressure."

Tiffany left in the Jeep, heading for downtown and breakfast with her father at the Empress. I was in the sunroom reading Danda Humphreys' history of Victoria street names when Hart appeared. He was wearing a white shirt and black trousers.

"Hey, Liz—remember saying you'd like to get aboard a cruise ship? Well, close that book, because your chance has come."

"Excellent."

We hurried outside. "Cruise ships dock at Ogden

Point," Hart explained. "We're invited aboard the *Crystal Paradise*."

At the estate's 10-car garage, Cambridge waited beside the Daimler. "Normally I'd ride my bicycle to Ogden Point," Hart said, as we settled back on the limo's luxurious leather seats, "but we're running very late. I slept in. It was a busy night."

"For me, too," I responded.

"Quickly, please," Hart said to Cambridge, who was at the wheel. "We're late."

Hart turned to me. "I belong to a service club called Victoria A.M. We promote local tourism—for example, by welcoming cruise ship passengers to Victoria."

"Why belong to a service club, when you're so wealthy?"

"It's important to give back to the community, Liz. Besides, I've got my own ecotourism business. I like talking shop with other members of Vic A.M."

"Pepper mentioned something about you greeting the cruise ships. Exactly what happens?"

"We give each lady a flower and each gentleman a handshake as they leave the ship."

"That sounds like fun."

"I've got permission for you to join us. I just made arrangements with Rachel and Bob, who organize our Meet and Greet Program. They've been married for 57 years. Mary Helmcken also may be there. Her family goes back to Sir James Douglas, the first governor of British Columbia."

"Cool—I'd love to meet her."

"You ladies will wear splendid dresses from the Edwardian period, and the gentlemen will be in top hats and evening suits. We'll get photographed a lot—wait and see."

"Has Tiffany ever done this? I bet she'd look gorgeous in one of those dresses."

"I've thought about inviting Tiff," Hart replied. "But she's engaged to Paris. It wouldn't be proper."

"I'll tell you something, Hart. I don't think Paris is right for Tiffany."

He turned to me, startled. "Really? Why's that?"

"Where do I begin? There are a million reasons. Haven't you noticed?"

"Sure, but . . ." A blush spread slowly across Hart's face. "But what would happen to Tiff? If she didn't marry Paris? What would she do? Where would she go?"

I smiled. "She'd think of something, I'm sure."

When the Daimler reached the Dallas Road cliffs, I looked for the *Outlaw,* but without success. Then I was distracted by the sight of the cruise ship docked at Ogden Point. Even from this distance it looked massive, looming over the dock and the red double-decker buses parked alongside many taxis and limousines for hire.

"Cruise ships stay in port all day," Hart explained, "so most passengers come ashore to sightsee."

At a small building near the wharf we changed into our costumes. The members of "Vic A.M." were a cheerful lot; I chatted with Rachel and Mary while their friend Flo helped adjust my elaborate hat and gown of crimson satin.

Hart and the other men walked with us to the ship; each of the ladies carried a basket of brightly coloured flowers. The cruise ship's bow shimmered with sunlight that reflected from the ocean waters, an impressive backdrop as we took photos of each other.

Cruise passengers waved to us from the many decks above. One of Victoria's famous hanging flower baskets was placed beside the gangplank for photo opportunities, and then the passengers descended.

At first I was timid, but the people were very friendly. "You look real English," said a man with a southern twang to his voice. "How about letting me get a photograph of you?"

I was impressed, listening to Flo speak in French to people from Québec and Europe. The others also kept busy, giving advice on what Victoria attractions to visit, plus constantly posing for photographs.

Then it was time to board the cruise ship!

We climbed the gangplank behind Tommy Mayne, a retired high school teacher who'd been energetically clanging a brass bell in his role as Victoria's town crier. Our identification was checked by a crew member at the top of the gangplank, and then we entered the ship's central atrium.

I looked up, surprised at the open and airy spaces above. In this large gathering place, passengers strolled or chatted with crew members; along one side, glass-enclosed elevators rose to the many upper decks. Bright waters streamed down a wall, framing a statue of a dancing couple. Nearby was a crystal piano—an amazing sight.

We began handing out flowers while answering questions from people curious about our outfits. The passengers came from many countries—and everyone said they'd like to live in Victoria. After posing for more pictures, we ascended a grand staircase that swept up to a collection of shops displaying expensive gowns, jewellery and perfumes.

Flo's husband, Eric, smiled at me. "Did you bring your platinum credit cards, Liz?"

"Unfortunately not," I laughed.

We chanced upon the ship's movie theatre, where a man slumbered alone amidst the empty seats. Flo took a picture and the flash woke the man, who looked around blearily. Giggling together, we scurried away.

The others were waiting for an elevator. When it arrived, we crowded inside. We adjusted our hats in front of the mirrors, while the elevator swiftly rose an amazing 11 stories to the Lido Deck.

Through a glass door I could see some people lounging beside a large swimming pool. We entered a restaurant where others were enjoying breakfast; when Tommy clanged the brass bell, they all jumped. Then everyone relaxed and smiled as we rushed around dispensing the last of our flowers. "Welcome to Canada's best bloomin' city," I kept saying—an expression I'd heard the others using.

Our duties complete, we received our treat—a late breakfast, courtesy of the cruise ship. The selection of delicacies was mind-boggling; we were offered 10 different juices, omelettes loaded with smoked salmon, fruit, link sausages, bacon—you name it.

Carrying trays laden with food, we went outside to the open deck. I took Flo and Eric's photograph beside a statue of a mermaid, then joined Hart, Les Chan, and Tommy at a round table. The others sat close by.

Munching our delicious breakfast, we enjoyed

Rachel's description of the deer she'd seen in her yard that morning. "Their coats were as sleek as this table-top," she said. "We even had a mom and two little spotted babies—they were so cute. I put out carrot peelings for them."

"We've had deer in our garden, too," Tommy said, "eating the tender leaves of the hydrangeas."

After finishing my meal I strolled to the railing, where I looked at the blue waters far below. A number of small boats had assembled, their occupants staring up at our mighty vessel.

Then my cell phone rang. It was William, sounding agitated.

"Liz," he exclaimed. "Can you meet me? I've made a decision—we must talk."

"Of course," I replied.

"Be outside the Royal B.C. Museum in one hour. I've got something really important to tell you."

* * *

Forty minutes later, Cambridge stopped the Daimler outside the museum, which was located near the Inner Harbour. "What a mob scene," I said, surprised at the number of people gathered on the large lawns outside the Legislative Buildings. They sat on rugs and aluminum chairs facing the water, where a barge had been anchored. "What's going on?"

"Later tonight," Hart explained, "the Victoria Symphony Orchestra will be on that barge, playing classical tunes. It's an annual event called the Symphony Splash. These people have arrived early, to get the best spots."

"I wouldn't mind attending," I said wistfully.

"Didn't anyone tell you? Major Wright has invited us all to watch thc Splash from his suite at the Empress. We'll have a choice view."

"Excellent!"

After waving goodbye to Hart and watching the Daimler drive off, I studied the museum. It was a large, handsome building of white stone. Through big windows I saw ancient totem poles that had been gathered long ago, perhaps from the very villages that Emily Carr captured in her books and paintings.

Then my heart lurched.

At the Inner Harbour I saw William—with someone else.

The two of them strolled arm in arm along Belleville; she looked pert and summery in a yellow dress and sun hat. Then, to my horror, I saw William hug the girl. As she hurried away, she turned to blow him a kiss.

I watched William walk toward the museum. I was horrified—frozen by indecision. I thought, *maybe she was in those photos that William scooped into hiding in his studio*. Pain stabbed me. I remembered seeing Hart with that pretty Lorna, who turned out to be family. Maybe this had the same explanation? Not likely, I thought bitterly.

William saw me and smiled. In the distance beyond him, I could still see that girl in her yellow dress. I really wished I'd never seen them together—I felt so down about it. I wanted to run, to escape the jealousy. It hurt so much.

As William approached, I produced a totally phony

smile. He looked surprised, but I didn't care. Bad vibrations ruled my heart.

"What's wrong?" William asked, looking at me with those wonderful eyes.

I refused to melt. "Nothing," I replied, giving him another frosty smile.

"Something's bothering you, Liz. Please, tell me what's wrong."

"Hey," I said, looking for a diversion, "this museum could be interesting. Let's take a look, okay?"

"Sure, but what's wrong?"

"Nothing much."

"Liz, there's something I need to tell you. That's why I asked to meet."

"Later, maybe," I replied. I was so sulky.

I felt terrible, especially when William fell into silence. I was quiet, too, lost in misery. We stepped onto an escalator; at the top, William turned to me. "Let's go see the woolly mammoth. It's my favourite exhibit."

"You go, William." I looked at my map of the museum. "I'm going to check out the First Peoples Gallery. It interests me more." I was lying—what I really needed was time alone, time to think. I'd never felt this way before. It was horrible.

"Okay," William said. "I'll meet you in the gallery. Wait for me, okay? I know you're angry, Liz, but don't walk out."

I watched William disappear around a corner. Instantly I felt alone, and awful. What monster of jealousy had seized my heart? I felt so guilty, and I badly needed to apologize.

Hurry back, *William*, I whispered anxiously.

I entered the First Peoples Gallery, where the lighting was dim. I was in a room designed to resemble a longhouse from the days when Native villages dominated the B.C. coast. I looked at the four totem poles supporting a wooden roof, trying to picture Emily Carr visiting a longhouse like this.

The gallery continued into a second large room containing many huge totems. Indirect lighting glowed discreetly, as did a red *Exit* sign over an emergency door. I studied a replica of a seaside village, complete with miniature canoes on a beach. The village looked perfect in every detail.

Then I saw William, reflected in the glass of the display case. He'd just entered the room.

William looked grim, but I wasn't surprised. I'd been really spiteful, and I couldn't wait to apologize. What to say? I stared at the miniature village, trying to find the right words. Then a loud buzzing distracted me, and a door slammed shut. Turning from the display, I looked for William.

But he wasn't there.

I searched the gallery, then walked quickly to the outside corridor. Tourists passed by, chattering happily. I couldn't see William—what was going on? Now I felt really bad about my sulky mood.

After rushing back inside the First Peoples Gallery, I hurried to the Modern History Gallery. I searched the face of every tall boy, unable to believe this was happening. I felt as if I'd entered a dream state, and I wanted to cry.

Entering a town from the Old West, I tried to decide

my next move. Happy people surrounded me, laughing and exclaiming as they wandered past the Grand Hotel and an old railway station and other exhibits.

At last I made a decision. After looking for William at the woolly mammoth, I left the museum. As enthused people hurried past, I took out my cell phone and called Laura Singlehurst.

"Please be home," I whispered, as her line rang and rang. "Don't let a machine answer."

Then Laura was there, her voice breathless. "I was outside, talking to the moving van guys. I ran to catch the phone—I thought it could be important."

"It is important," I cried, as tears rolled from my eyes. "Oh, Laura, please come get me. I'm at the Royal B.C. Museum, and I'm so frightened. Please drive me home, so I can talk to you."

"I'll be right there."

True to her word, Laura soon pulled up in a bright red Cadillac. "This is a rental," she explained, opening the door for me. "I've sold the BMW."

I told Laura everything. "I was so sulky," I moaned. "What if I never see William again? I was horrible to him!"

Laura patted my hand sympathetically. "There must be a simple explanation. What about the emergency exit at the gallery? You heard the door slam shut."

"You mean, William left that way?"

"He could have," Laura replied. "I think maybe his feelings are hurt, but he'll come back. Wait and see."

"I should contact the police."

"Not yet," Laura said. "Wait at least 24 hours, in case William shows up."

Soon Thirteen Oaks appeared ahead. At the front door of the mansion, I quickly thanked Laura, then ran inside. I was longing for a message from William.

But there was nothing. Alone in my room, I broke down and cried and cried.

* * *

Two hours later, Tiff returned home. In her room, I confessed my foolishness.

She listened sympathetically.

"What are your instincts saying?" she asked.

"To trust William."

"There's your answer. He'll return, don't you worry." Tiffany sighed. "I'm getting married tomorrow," she moaned, "and meanwhile Paris insists that we attend the Symphony Splash this evening after the rehearsal. But I just don't want to."

"Then, don't go, Tiffany."

"Paris doesn't want to upset my father. Daddy has invited us to his suite at the Empress overlooking the Splash activities. Everyone has to attend."

"I'm not going," I declared. "I'm too upset about William."

"Maybe he'll be at the Splash," Tiffany suggested.

"That's a thought. But what if he's with that girl?"

"Then the truth will set you free."

"I don't want freedom," I murmured sadly. "I want William."

Late in the day we attended the wedding rehearsal at the castle. The Major kept checking his watch, probably feeling impatient about the 24 hours still remaining until his daughter became Lady deMornay.

After the rehearsal Pepper returned home with her baby, who was fussy and maybe coming down with something. Major Wright left early in a taxi for the Empress Hotel. When the rehearsal ended, the rest of us crowded into the Daimler. I was squeezed in beside Kate Partridge, maid of honour to Tiffany. Kate lived in Victoria, and told some funny stories about the city as we drove downtown. The classic limousine attracted a lot of stares. Crowds of people were on the sidewalks, carrying lawn chairs and blankets toward the Inner Harbour.

"They'll never find a place to sit," Cambridge predicted from the wheel. "Forty thousand are expected for the Symphony Splash. According to CBC Radio, people started arriving at dawn to pick a good location."

We stepped from the limousine on Douglas Street. "Please, wait for me," Tiffany said to Cambridge. "I'll be back in a few minutes, and I'd appreciate a ride home."

Cambridge touched his chauffeur's cap. "Very good, miss."

Hart looked disappointed. "What's wrong, Tiffany?"

"Too many things to do," she replied. "Hey, tomorrow night I'm getting married."

Paris smiled at her. "Your father's going to be upset. I bet he'll have other guests, all anxious to chat with his perfect daughter."

"Well," Tiff replied, "that's just too bad."

A security guard checked our identification, then admitted us to the Victoria Convention Centre, which adjoins the Empress Hotel. We hurried past a magnificent indoor totem pole and climbed a few stairs to the hotel, where the reception would be held after the wedding.

I looked at Tiffany. "You're missing the Splash? Won't your father mind?"

"Maybe," Tiffany replied. She looked scared; she was breathing deeply as we entered an elevator and rode up. We stepped out into a hallway—it was very wide, with portraits of British royalty on the walls. Major Wright waited at the door of his suite; at his side was a woman I recognized. She'd been on the carriage ride with the Major.

"This is Marjorie," the Major said. "We met last week—we were both taking tea in the lobby. Marjorie's in Victoria on holiday from Texas." He beamed at Tiffany. "Marjorie's my date for this century's most romantic event."

"I enjoy high-society weddings," Marjorie told me. Stepping closer, she lowered her voice. "The deMornay family is, of course, *very* high society."

Tiffany looked at her father. "Daddy, I'm not staying for the Splash. I'm going home."

"Nonsense," the Major replied. "Come into the suite."

"But, Daddy, I'm getting married tomorrow."

"Please, honey. This is important to me."

"Daddy, I'm sorry. I can't stay."

Tiff quickly told me and Kate goodbye, then rushed toward the elevators. The Major took a step in her direction, then stopped. Glancing at Marjorie, he faked a jolly grin. "Kids these days."

Paris looked at him. "It's just pre-wedding jitters, Major Wright. Nothing to worry about."

"Let's hope so," the Major replied.

His large suite overlooked the Inner Harbour. Laura was there, along with several of the Major's Winnipeg friends, in town for the wedding. We exchanged handshakes and small talk, then I finally rushed into the adjoining room. I'd brought binoculars from Thirteen Oaks and was anxious to scan the crowd for William. With forty thousand in attendance my chances were slim, but I had to try.

From the window I saw an enchanting scene—the evening sun was a golden sphere that reflected from the blue waters of the harbour and threw long shadows behind the people who crowded the lawns below.

Laura joined me, carrying a platter of food. "The crab sandwiches are delicious," she said. "Or try the *paté de foie gras*. The taste is heavenly."

"Thanks, Laura, but I'm not hungry."

"No news about William?"

I shook my head mournfully. "Nothing."

"I'm so sorry, Liz."

The harbour was dominated by the barge where the symphony would play. On the water, music lovers had assembled to listen in canoes and motorboats, kayaks and cruisers. The shore was dense with people, and they covered every available spot as far as the distant steps of the Legislative Buildings.

"This is hopeless," I said, training the binoculars on the crowd. "William could be anywhere."

In the distance a helicopter lifted off from Ogden Point and moved slowly toward the Inner Harbour, sunlight glinting from its whirling blades. "Sight-seers," Laura said. "They've paid a lot of money for a bird's-eye view of this scene. A friend of Hart's owns that helicopter company."

On the barge, the members of the Victoria Symphony Orchestra warmed up their instruments. Then these sounds stopped, and we heard the opening notes of "O Canada." Immediately the spectators stood up, on the lawns and the streets and out on the bigger boats, to sing the national anthem.

The concert began with a rousing selection that received a huge cheer from the enthusiastic crowd. Then people nodded along to Bizet's "Carmen Suite" and Gershwin's "Fascinating Rhythm." But the big hit was a solo performance of a Mozart piano concerto by Victoria's 12-year-old Samuel Seong, who exhibited great self-confidence.

During the intermission we watched the Canadian Scottish Regiment march proudly past to the rattle of drums and the skirl of bagpipes. Glow ropes had appeared in the crowd, their neon colours beautiful in the gathering darkness; I saw a young Splash volunteer and another boy having a mock sword fight with lime green glow ropes.

With the binoculars I scanned the crowd, hoping, always hoping. Laura returned from the other room, auburn hair swinging. "There'll be some great music after the intermission," she said, "followed by the grand finale. It's the '1812 Overture,' Tchaikovsky's celebration of a famous Russian military victory over Napoleon's armies. It was written to be performed outside, with the loud ringing of church bells and the sound of cannons adding to the victorious music. The music went immediately to number one on the classical charts, and it's been popular ever since. It's rousing, cheerful stuff." She smiled at me. "We'll hear bells and cannons tonight, followed by fireworks."

"It sounds wonderful, Laura. I just wish William was here."

"Don't worry about that other girl, Liz."

"Thanks, Laura. I'll try not to."

Laura went to visit with Kate and Marjorie, the Major's friend from the United States, and I scanned the crowd with the binoculars. Hart joined me for a talk, and then Paris appeared. He dropped into a nearby chair and flipped through the pages of a magazine.

I tried the crowd again with the binoculars. "Oh, my goodness, there he is!"

11

Hart leaned close to the window. "William?"

"No, that kid Jason. The one from the *Outlaw*. He's beside the statue of Captain Cook—I'd know him anywhere."

I handed the binoculars to Hart. "I'm going down there. First that guy took a shot at us. After that, he firebombed the *Amor*, then he stole the painting and returned it. I want to know what's going on."

"Let me go with you."

I shook my head. "No thanks, Hart. I've got my cell phone, and I'll be perfectly safe in that big crowd. I work best on my own."

"How can I reach you?"

I gave Hart my cell number, then thanked Major Wright for his hospitality. After explaining my mission to Laura, I hurried to the elevator, took it down, and left the Empress. Jason was across the crowded street, holding a cell phone against his ear; suddenly he snapped it shut, and surveyed the crowd with suspicious eyes.

Then he was gone, down the stone stairs beside Cook's statue. Shouting for him to stop, I hurried forward through the crowd.

At the statue I groaned in dismay. On the causeway below was a solid wall of humanity; using brute strength, Jason was forcing a path through the crowd. People shook their fists after him, as parents comforted wailing toddlers and others expressed disgust in loud voices, but Jason just kept moving. Only once did he pause, when he turned to wave up at someone in the Empress.

All around were the rich sounds of powerful music. Without my noticing, the concert had resumed. I looked up at the hotel, searching for the Major's suite. All vehicles had been banned from the immediate vicinity, so the wide expanse of Government Street was filled with strolling people, many speaking foreign languages.

I walked south through the throng, envying people their happiness. Seeing the Royal B.C. Museum, I remembered my last moments with William. He'd have loved this scene—the night air was festive and the musicians on the brightly lit barge looked so spectacular, all of them wearing white.

People were clapping in time, while others bopped around to a Sousa march, a favourite of my dad's. I smiled sadly, wishing my family were here. I could have used my brother's help with this investigation, but he was on summer holidays with his pal, the odious Dietmar Oban.

My cell phone went *ta-ta-tring-tring*. It was Hart calling. "Are you okay, Liz?"

"Yes."

"That's good. Any sign of Jason?"

"I lost him in the crowd."

"Too bad. Listen," Hart continued, abruptly changing the subject, "I've got news you'll like. A friend just called, offering you a free seat on tonight's final helicopter tour. Cambridge is waiting with the Daimler outside the Crystal Garden. He'll take you there, but hurry."

Immediately I took off running toward the corner of Douglas and Belleville. "What's with the chopper?" I asked Hart as I ran with my phone.

"My friend owns it. Someone cancelled their trip, and he offered me seats."

"I hope you're coming along," I shouted into the phone, running hard toward the Daimler. I saw Cambridge waiting, the door already open.

"No thanks," Hart replied. "There isn't enough time."

"Thanks for the opportunity!"

The drive didn't take long. The helicopter waited near the wharf where we'd visited the cruise ship; it resembled a large insect with its giant blades and large windows. For a moment I imagined spotting William from the chopper, but even with binoculars he'd be impossible to see from up that high.

To my surprise, Cambridge asked for permission to join the trip. "Sure thing," the pilot replied. "There's enough space."

When the helicopter lifted off, I was unexpectedly reminded of what happened when I was a hostage at Disneyland. Closing my eyes, I pictured hot-tempered Serena Hernandez, and how she behaved. It was a horrible memory.

When I opened my eyes a few moments later, I saw people below in their yards and on apartment balconies, watching the sky for the coming fireworks. I sat in the best seat, beside the pilot. She smiled at me.

"We'll reach the Empress exactly as the '1812 Overture' concludes. Watch for the cannons to fire."

Far below we saw the fairy lights that decorated the Legislative Buildings, and the streets twinkling all the way to the ocean at Oak Bay. On the water, the orchestra's bandshell shone brightly.

Beside the Inner Harbour, orange flames exploded from cannons. "Those guns are fired by sailors from HMCS *Quadra*," the pilot told us. "They're antique cannons, brought to Victoria each summer for the Symphony Splash. They're firing blanks, of course."

A sudden explosion burst in the sky, scattering colours. "The fireworks," the pilot exclaimed, looking at the bright jewels exploding in the night. "Oh, aren't they beautiful!" It was thrilling to watch the eruptions of fire and light from here, and I kept wishing William could see this incredible scene.

Then, too soon, it was over, and numerous headlights sprang to life all around the Inner Harbour.

"There'll be a traffic jam tonight," Cambridge predicted gloomily. "Just the thing to set off Master Paris's bad temper."

Our helicopter headed south over the slumbering

trees of Beacon Hill Park. In the distance I saw the outline of the Olympic Mountains; close by, the Dallas Road cliffs overlooked the shoreline.

"Wait a minute," I said, sitting up straight. "Look at that boat—it could be the *Outlaw*. Can we get closer?"

The pilot glanced at her watch. "There's time, if—"

"No," Cambridge said sharply. "We must return immediately to Ogden Point."

"But," I pleaded, "surely . . ."

"My name is not Shirley," Cambridge replied crossly, "and I haven't got time to waste on a wild-goose chase. Master Paris will expect the limousine back at the Empress Hotel. He'll be furious if we're late."

It was hopeless to argue, and I watched sadly as the boat disappeared in the direction of Oak Bay. It could have been the *Outlaw*, but how would I ever know?

* * *

The next day was terrible.

I tried and tried to reach William by phone, without success. As for Tiffany, she sat at her window, gazing out to sea. I couldn't get her to talk, and she looked a misery.

At seven p.m., the wedding party gathered in the drawing room at Craigdarroch Castle. A marriage commissioner was there to perform the ceremony. Paris deMornay looked so smug; he wore a white tuxedo, and so did Hart, who was best man. They stood with us in front of the white fireplace, awaiting the arrival of the bride. A couple of dozen guests sat in chairs, glancing expectantly toward the door. When would Tiffany arrive?

From outside the panelled oak doors, we heard an organ play the opening bars of "Here Comes the Bride." Laura and the other guests stood up. The bride appeared, and my heart just about stood still; her downcast eyes were puffy from tears.

Beside Tiffany was the Major. Wearing an expensive suit and shiny shoes, he bristled with nervous energy. His eyebrows twitched as his blue eyes flicked from face to face. Father and daughter walked slowly forward, with Tiffany's eyes still on the floor.

I glanced at Paris; he grinned in satisfaction, his white teeth gleaming. Hart looked extremely unhappy, but he was a gentleman and would never dream of stopping the ceremony.

For a wild moment I thought I should do something—maybe yell, *Tiffany, don't,* and just see what happened. But I remained silent as the commissioner asked, "Who gives this woman?" and the Major presented Tiffany as a gift to Paris.

The ceremony commenced. Blood drummed in my ears throughout the long and terrible time; at moments I feared I'd fall on the floor in a dead faint. Paris promised his bride he'd love, honour, and respect (what a lie), and then the commissioner turned to Tiffany for her pledge.

Taking a deep breath, my friend looked at Paris. "I can't do this," she said quietly.

He frowned. "What?"

Tiffany swallowed. "I always loved you, Paris. But I can't go down this road with you."

Paris continued to frown but said nothing.

"You're doing stuff that is so damaging. Money is your god—and before, it never was." Now Tiffany's voice was clear; everyone could hear the words. "You're being so reckless, Paris, taking such chances."

"I doubt it," Paris said, but his voice lacked conviction.

"You know what's the worst thing, Paris? Other people get hurt by your shady deals, and you don't care. In fact, you don't even notice. Even when it's family like Hart and Pepper, and me."

"Okay, Tiffany, okay. Message received. Now let's get married, eh? The commissioner's waiting, and so's everyone else."

Paris took Tiffany by the arm, but she pulled free. "It's not going to happen, Paris. Wedding bells aren't ringing for us."

Fear crept into his eyes. "Tiffany, please." Paris pleadingly reached out a hand. "We both need this marriage."

Major Wright was staring at Tiffany from his seat in the front row. "What's going on?" he demanded. His friend Marjorie patted the Major's arm, trying to keep him calm, but he ignored her. "What's going on?" he repeated.

"Daddy, I can't. I don't love Paris anymore."

The Major stood up. He looked broken-hearted. "Tiffany, honey, what's the matter? Of course you're going to marry Paris. He's a great guy. Now listen, you're just having an attack of nerves. Don't worry, just—"

Tiffany put her roses into my hands. "I was going to throw you this bouquet, Liz, so you'd be the next one married. Now I can't."

I felt radiant with joy. Hugging Tiffany close, I whispered, "I'm so proud of you, Tiff. Now get out of here—before you change your mind!"

Paris grabbed Tiffany's arm. "Please," he begged, "don't leave me. I'm sorry for the times I hurt you. It'll never happen again, Tiffany. Don't leave—I love you."

"You liar." Tiffany shook off his hand. She looked wonderful—so defiant and proud. "You love money, Paris. You won't get mine now."

Then my friend was gone, out the door to freedom. Major Wright's jaw hung open, and Paris looked totally astonished, but the room hummed with excitement. The guests hadn't expected this!

Pepper rushed to me. "Wasn't Tiffany *wonderful*? That took such bravery—my brother is a first-class power tripper."

"I'm so glad she found the courage," I said.

Pepper beamed with happiness. "Hey, what about the cruise? What'll happen now?"

"You're right," I said. "I'd completely forgotten."

Major Wright had booked a luxury suite on a cruise ship to Alaska. That was his wedding gift—Paris and Tiffany were supposed to sail tonight at midnight. Now the Major was stuck with the suite—but I figured he could afford it.

* * *

Outside the castle, the wedding guests were still murmuring excitedly. I watched Major Wright speaking urgently to Paris as they climbed into the Daimler.

Hart and Marjorie joined them, and the limo zoomed away.

"They've forgotten us," I said to Pepper.

"Too much on their minds."

After talking a while with the other guests, we took a taxi together to Thirteen Oaks. Pepper went in search of Amanda, and I changed out of my bridesmaid's dress. Then I looked for Tiffany.

I found her in a chair, looking out at the sea. "Hey," I said, "I bet you're the talk of Victoria."

"I'm worried about Daddy," Tiff replied. "The wedding meant so much to him."

"He'll get over it," I said, sitting down beside her. "Why'd you change your mind?"

"Laura told me to ask my angels to give me direction. So I spent today thinking about Paris. He's been clinging to me like a weight, hoping I'd solve his problems. I need an equal partner to help raise a family, not some guy who acts like he's drowning. He's an okay guy, Liz, but the wrong guy for me." Tiffany sighed. "Paris slipped into some bad habits after losing his dad. I tried to help—it's my nature, I guess. But I felt like his mother or something, getting him through crisis after crisis."

"You put more money into his gambling?"

Tiffany nodded. "Paris used up all his financial resources trying to maintain his reputation as a party-on dude. He borrowed big-time from all his friends. Then he turned to gambling to fix things. Now everything's dried up, and Paris will hit the wall."

"He'll survive," I predicted. "You wait and see."

* * *

Later that night, Tiffany was summoned by her father to the cruise ship. She asked me to go along for support, and we drove downtown in the Daimler, with Cambridge at the wheel.

The cruise ship looked beautiful, its sleek white lines dominating the busy night at Ogden Point. Taxis and limos and tour buses were delivering passengers for the midnight sailing of the *Romance of the Seas*. From the many decks above, faces looked down at the bustling scene.

After the Daimler pulled away, we climbed the gangplank. I felt worried about Tiffany, wondering if she'd still cave in. The Major was skilled at using emotional power to control his daughter.

"What's going on?" I asked Tiffany, as our identification was checked at the top of the gangplank. "Why has your dad summoned you here?"

She shook her blonde curls. "I don't know, Liz."

A young ship's officer was waiting for us with a personal welcome, and escorted us into a glass-enclosed elevator. We rose rapidly, looking down at clusters of passengers below. From the elevator we entered the Royal Deck, where the corridor was wide and deep purple carpeting pampered our feet. Each cabin had a name; at one called Suite of Dreams, the officer knocked discreetly.

"Major Wright," he called. "Your daughter has arrived."

The door opened. The Major's blue eyes stared at us, then he turned to the officer. "Thank you."

The officer saluted.

"Come inside," the Major snapped. "Marjorie's here. She's going to be a witness."

"To what?" Tiffany asked.

The Major didn't reply. I goggled at the size and luxury of the suite; there was even a large outdoor balcony with a panoramic view of the ocean and mountains. Marjorie sat on a luxurious sofa; in her hand was a fizzy drink.

"Good evening, girls," she said brightly, nervous eyes on Major Wright.

Hands on hips, he stared at Tiffany. She held his gaze without flinching. "Well, young lady?" the Major demanded. "Where is your apology?"

"Daddy, I—"

"Because," the Major continued, "tonight I am the laughing stock of Victoria society, and it is your fault, young lady."

"No, Daddy. If you hadn't—"

Again the Major interrupted his daughter. "Never mind," he barked. "There will be no further discussion."

Opening his cell phone, the Major punched some numbers. "What's your ETA?" he said into the phone. "Remember—this ship sails at midnight." Snapping shut the phone, the Major gestured at Tiffany. "Go sit with Marjorie and have a chat."

My friend did as ordered. I stepped out on the balcony and sniffed the salty air. Far below, the scene was active; I watched the scurrying ant-like figures, then saw a taxi pull to a stop.

Paris stepped out and hurried toward the ship; with him was Hart deMornay—and the marriage commissioner.

12

Quickly I returned inside. The deMornay brothers entered the suite, and Paris soon stood waiting to resume the marriage ceremony. The Major turned to Tiffany. "Sweetie, please, do this for your dear old pop. Call me a sentimental old fool, but just think what this marriage means."

"Daddy, I—"

Major Wright stopped her with a gesture. "I have this wonderful vision of my little girl marrying into the aristocracy. Surely that's not asking too much."

Tiffany smiled fondly at her father. "I know, Daddy, but face up to it. I will not marry Paris. That's my decision, and I won't change it."

Paris walked slowly toward Tiffany. I saw tears in his eyes. "Sweetheart, is there no way we can work this out?"

Tiffany shook her head. "No, Paris. My mind's made up."

"But . . ."

Tiffany turned to me. "Come on, Liz, let's get going."

Outside in the corridor, we walked rapidly toward the elevators. From behind, Paris called Tiff's name. "I'll take this cruise to Alaska alone," he threatened.

"I guess that's up to Daddy," Tiffany replied.

"I'll meet someone better than you."

"Good luck to her," Tiffany muttered, jabbing at the elevator button. "As for me, I'm out of here."

The elevator door opened, and I saw a young guy wearing a FedEx messenger's uniform. In his hands was a large metal tube. As we entered the elevator, I saw the messenger knock on the door of a suite.

* * *

Back at the estate we found Pepper in the library reading R.S.S. Wilson's *Undercover for the RCMP*. The baby was asleep upstairs. When Pepper heard about the events on board the cruise ship, her eyes glowed.

"You're something else, Tiff."

"Thanks, Pepper."

Looking exhausted, Tiffany left for bed. I stood at the library window, staring out at the ocean. Then, feeling weary and starting to cry, I dropped down on the sofa beside Pepper. "I'm so tired," I said, wiping away my tears. "Everything's just so horrible."

"What's wrong, Liz? What's happened?"

I was surprised. "You haven't heard?"

"About what?"

"I can't believe no one has told you, Pepper. I just assumed . . ."

"Told me what?" Pepper demanded impatiently.

"That my friend William has disappeared."

"*What?*"

Pepper was terribly upset by the news. She stared at me in horror as I described everything, starting from when I spotted William and the girl outside the museum.

Then Pepper leaned toward me. "Liz, I may know where William is."

"What do you mean?"

Pepper looked out the window. "William could be on Hidden Island."

"But why?"

Jumping up from the sofa, Pepper paced the library. There were tears in her eyes. "Liz, you've been so kind. Most people see a kid with a baby and turn up their noses. You and Tiff—that's not your style. You're good people."

"Thanks, Pepper, but what's this all about?"

She took a deep breath. "I helped steal the painting, Liz. I was the inside person. I gave the code to Jason."

"But, Pepper!"

"Liz, I had no idea that William was missing. It was strange to see him with Jason, but I didn't think anything more about it."

"What are you talking about?"

She stared at me with solemn eyes. "Jason's been hiding out in an abandoned boathouse on Hidden Island. Yesterday I saw his boat heading there—William was with him. You know my story about the unexploded bombs? It's not true—I made that up. I wanted to keep people off the island. That way, it's my private property."

"But, Pepper, why'd you give the code to Jason?"

"I was promised enough money to start my recording studio, so I agreed to help."

"Jason was going to pay you?"

Pepper shook her head. "No. We're both working for someone else."

"Who?"

"I can't tell you, Liz."

"But why steal the *Klee Wyck* and then return it?"

Pepper looked at the painting over the fireplace. The colours were so pleasing, the Laughing One so happy. "Because that's not the real *Klee Wyck*," she replied at last. "That's a forgery, a fake."

I was astonished. "But it looks so real!"

"You see, Liz, I told Jason the security code, and unlocked an outside door for him to get into the house. Jason escaped with the *Klee Wyck*. Then some forger made an expert copy, which you were lured into finding at Butchart Gardens. That was so everyone would relax, thinking the painting was safe."

I shook my head. "Why make a copy?"

"So the original can be sold, for major money."

"But where's the original?"

"Until tonight," Pepper replied, "it's been right here at Thirteen Oaks. After you found the forged copy at Butchart Gardens, Jason gave the original to me. I've kept it hidden here until now."

"So you think William's on that island? Then we must go there immediately."

"No problem," Pepper said. "There's an underground

tunnel from the library to Hidden Island. Nobody knows about the tunnel, including Jason. I didn't want him getting into our house."

"You didn't mind him stealing the *Klee Wyck*?"

Pepper shrugged. "Who cares, it's just some old painting. Besides, no one noticed the forgery. Paris, Hart—everyone was fooled. Remember the family meeting with Laura? Major Wright and the others—they all said how beautiful it looked." She shook her head, looking amused. "They were all fooled, every one."

"Including me," I said ruefully. "But that painting was so special to your father, Tiff. Didn't that bother you?"

Pepper snapped her fingers disdainfully. "Not even this much," she declared. "You know, when my father crashed the car and killed my wonderful mother, he was driving drunk. I'll never forgive him." Pepper gazed defiantly at me with those beautiful deMornay eyes. "No, Liz, I don't have any trouble about the painting being forged."

"You've been paid for helping?"

Pepper shook her head. "Not until the original is sold."

"Who's paying you, Pepper? Who's your boss?"

She shook her head. "I can't tell you, Liz. Please, don't ask."

I thought of another question. This one made me feel sick, but I had to ask. "What's William got to do with Jason?"

"I have no idea, Liz."

I decided not to press the issue. I had to find

William, and this was the closest I'd come so far. "Okay, then," I said. "How can we reach that tunnel?"

Moments later Pepper opened the library's secret panel; I smelled wetness and dirt. We stepped into a tunnel. As the false bookcase closed behind us, Pepper switched on a flashlight. "This tunnel's where I hid the painting," she said, "inside a metal tube. Then tonight a FedEx driver collected the tube from me. I was glad to see it go."

I remembered seeing the FedEx messenger delivering a metal tube. "Did he take it to the *Romance of the Seas*?"

"Yes."

"Pepper, tell me something. Tiff and I were reading a book in the library, then the book disappeared. Did you take it?"

She nodded. Her flashlight beam crawled through the black air to land on the book called *History of Thirteen Oaks*. "It describes this tunnel," Pepper explained, "and how to open the secret panel. I didn't want you discovering the tunnel, Liz. You're a detective—things could've gone wrong. I heard you and Tiff from the hallway, talking about the book. I tricked you out of the library, with a fib about Jason phoning."

I nodded.

"Remember when I made lemonade?" Pepper asked. "Before I did, I raced to the library, opened the secret panel, and hid the book inside the tunnel."

"I thought maybe Jason had stolen the book, while I waited for his call at the office." I paused, thinking. "I remember at FolkFest you asked if I had any suspects."

"I was so glad you hadn't figured it out."

Our voices echoed in the shadowy darkness. I put a finger to my lips, warning Pepper against speaking; I was worried that Jason might hear. My heart thumped noisily and blood rushed inside my ears, but I refused to stop—I was determined to find William.

The tunnel was scary. Enclosed by wet and dripping stone, we stumbled over loose rocks, hearing the noise magnified a thousand times. I kept thinking we'd step on a rat, and I was so thankful when our underground journey finally ended.

I could smell the ocean as we exited the tunnel, stepping onto a grassy slope. "I disguised the tunnel mouth," Pepper told me proudly.

"You did a good job," I commented. "No one would ever figure there's a tunnel here."

In the moonlight I saw the boathouse below; it was overgrown with weeds, and part of the roof had collapsed. "What's in that shack?" I asked Pepper. "The one beside the boathouse."

"Junk. Abandoned outboard motors and oars, that kind of stuff."

"Switch off the flashlight," I cautioned, "in case Jason's around."

Cautiously we descended the slope toward the boathouse. Nothing moved except the waves, thumping against the island's rocky shoreline. A bird cried a warning over the ocean, then the night fell silent.

At the boathouse we peered through a filthy window. The big double doors were open to the sea: the *Outlaw* wasn't there. "I've watched Jason's boat from my room," Pepper said. "He usually goes out around this time, for about an hour. He painted out the name, but I know it's the *Outlaw*. I figure Jason gets bored and goes for a ride."

At the shack we found the lock wedged shut with a chunk of wood. Carefully I worked it loose, then reached for the handle. As the door squealed open on rusty hinges, moonlight flowed into the shack.

William lay on the floor, his arms and legs bound with rope.

I rushed to him, very worried. His eyes were open, but he seemed weak and confused; I cradled him gently in my arms, as Pepper released the ropes.

William tried to stand—he seemed very shaky. "Liz," he whispered, "it's so good to see you. But how did you find me?"

"It's not important right now," I replied. "Let's get you out of here."

"Wait. I've got a confession to make. I'm so ashamed."

"What do you mean?"

"Remember I asked you to meet me at the museum? When I had something to tell you?"

"Of course I remember. I behaved so badly."

"Well," William said, his voice only a whisper. "I . . . I'm a forger. I copied the *Klee Wyck*."

* * *

I was shocked. Since Pepper had broken the news, I'd never considered who the forger might be. I guess I was too intent on finding William. "You were partners with Jason?" I asked, dreading the answer. Had I been so wrong about William?

"Nothing like that," he replied, shaking his head. He was slowly coming around. "I was paid for doing a job. Jason offered good money for an Emily Carr forgery, no questions asked. When I copied the original *Klee Wyck,* I had no idea who owned it. I only learned the truth after Jason kidnapped me."

"At the Dallas Road seawall, someone in a low-rider truck gave you money. Was that Jason?"

William nodded.

"How'd you get hooked up with him?"

"He'd been hired by some local who wanted to steal an Emily Carr and get it forged by me. Jason offered a lot of cash. I figured, why not? I desperately needed the money."

I turned to Pepper. "Did you know any of this?"

"No, and I can't believe it," she responded. "I had no idea William made the forgery."

"But the fake note at Butchart Gardens was signed with a W, as in William." I looked closely at Pepper. "Did you write the note?"

She shook her head. "My boss did. My job was to get the note delivered to you at Butchart Gardens. But I might have mentioned William to my boss. I honestly can't remember."

I was getting worried that Jason might show up, but I needed more answers.

I turned back to William. "Jason paid up?"

He nodded. "After the original was stolen, I received my first payment. Jason later delivered the *Klee Wyck* to my studio so I could produce the forgery. When he collected the finished product, I got the remaining money."

"Why'd you need it, William? To finance getting your mom to Arizona?"

William nodded. "But she turned me down. When I told Mom about the forgery, she called it dirty money. So I phoned Jason. I said I planned to go to the police. He laughed and said I was a criminal myself, a forger. I hesitated about the police, for just a moment too long. Jason grabbed me."

"Jason phoned when Tiff and I visited your studio?"

William nodded.

"What were those—" I stopped myself. "No, forget it. I don't want to even think about it."

"You know," William said, "it was so horrible when Jason said he'd attacked you in the cemetery. He—"

"Jason?" I exclaimed. "He's the guy who attacked me?"

William nodded. "I'm just so glad you didn't get hurt. Jason told me later about the attack—he was trying to scare you off, stop your investigation."

"Did you know where Jason hid out? Did you know Pepper was involved?"

"No to both," William replied. "I didn't even know why the forgery." Lifting his head, William looked shyly at me. "Liz, will you forgive me?"

There was no question. William wasn't a criminal, out for personal gain. He'd exercised bad judgement, but anyone might. "Of course I understand, William. Besides, you should forgive me! I was such a shrew. I was jealous because I saw you hugging someone."

"At the Inner Harbour? Before I met you at the museum?"

I nodded.

"That was my sister, Lucille. We'd had a visit, and she was going to work. Lucille was late, or I'd have introduced you."

"I'm sorry," I said glumly. "What a jerk I was."

I turned to Pepper. "Let's get William back to the house, then call for an ambulance and the police."

We left the shack, and William moved slowly up the slope. When we reached the tunnel, I looked at Pepper. "Help William to the mansion, okay? I'll join you there."

"But—" William protested.

"No arguments," I said, gently kissing him. "I'll be okay."

The moment they disappeared into the tunnel, I hurried to the boathouse. After the *Outlaw* returned, I planned to sabotage the engine so Jason couldn't escape from the island.

Inside the boathouse I smelled engine fuel. A sleeping bag lay on the small wharf; nearby was a jumbled heap of clothes and junk food wrappers. Empty cans of pop and beer were scattered around.

Raising my head, I listened to the night. Was that an engine I heard? I looked out the open doors of the boathouse, wondering if Jason was returning. Moonlight lay across the waters, where nothing moved but sea birds on the wing.

Then I saw the lights of a boat, heading my way.

I slipped into hiding behind a big oil drum; the wharf was slippery, the wood stained by oil from the drum. Safely concealed, I watched the boat approach. Jason was at the controls at the open stern, guiding the boat's passage toward the boathouse.

Jason secured the *Outlaw* and hurried from the boathouse. He carried food, perhaps for William. My time was short. Scuttling out of hiding, I climbed down a wooden ladder to the deck of the *Outlaw*. For a moment I watched the door, fearing Jason's return, and then I hurried inside the deckhouse. Looking around, I saw a table, a small galley with basic cooking supplies, and steps leading down to the engine. Fortunately it wasn't covered, making my task that much easier.

As I reached for the engine's distributor cap, though, my luck ran out. I felt a gun in my back and heard Jason's chuckle. "Turn around slowly, you little fool."

* * *

Jason's nose seemed once to have been broken, and his tiny eyes glittered. He licked his lips. "Yum, yum. You're cute up close."

"You're not," I declared defiantly. "William has escaped, and you're finished. The cops are on their way."

"Then, let's be gone. Go out on deck. William was my hostage, but you'll do as a replacement."

I did as ordered. Keeping his nickel-plated revolver pointed at me, Jason released the mooring lines and started the boat's engine. I looked for a way to escape, but it was hopeless; I figured Jason wouldn't hesitate to use the gun on me. Now I wished I'd returned to the house with Pepper and William instead of playing the hero—but it was too late for regrets.

"I know all about the forgery," I said, hoping to rattle Jason. "I even know where the original is."

"So do I—it's on board the *Romance of the Seas*.

My boss plans to take it to some crooked collector in Alaska. The collector's ready to pay top dollar for Emily Carr's unknown masterpiece."

The *Outlaw* rumbled out of the boathouse, turned into the wind, and picked up speed. Above the shoreline I saw the Thirteen Oaks mansion; I prayed that William and Pepper had reached safety.

"My boss made me hang around," Jason said, "waiting for my payoff. Then I figured, why not get all the money, not just my payment but every single penny. That painting's got to be worth at least a million bucks."

"You're not only dangerous," I said. "You're greedy, too."

Jason laughed. He stood at the outdoor wheel; I sat on a wooden bench, huddled in my jacket against the cold wind. "The *Romance of the Seas* left port at midnight," Jason said. "We're going to board it and grab that painting. I'll take it to Alaska and get the money myself."

"Are you some kind of hired gun?"

"That's right," Jason replied proudly.

He cranked up the RPMs, and the shoreline rapidly grew smaller. I could no longer see the mansion at Thirteen Oaks. Shivering, I hugged myself tightly.

"I was hired," Jason said, "to get the *Klee Wyck* forged. Your friend William did a great job, then he developed cold feet. He wanted to return the money. I got to thinking, what if he went to the cops?"

Jason looked at me. "I saw you once with William. You took a bus home to the Uplands, and I followed in my truck. Then I kept an eye on Thirteen Oaks, waiting my chance. I figured I'd hurt you, as a warning to William."

"I notice you're limping," I commented.

"Yeah, thanks to you," Jason muttered. "I decided to kidnap William, in case I needed a hostage. I followed him into the First Peoples Gallery at the museum, and said a bomb was strapped around my waist. I threatened to blow up the place unless he left with me." Jason's laugh was unpleasant. "William figured I was crazy enough to be a suicide bomber, so he obeyed. We stepped through the emergency exit, escaped from the museum, and went straight to the *Outlaw* at the Inner Harbour. William came along quiet and peaceful, because he was afraid people would get hurt."

Jason sighed. "It was boring at Hidden Island, so I went to the Splash for something to do. That's when you spotted me, but I got a warning from my boss and escaped in time."

"Just exactly who is this boss of yours?"

"Fat chance I'd tell you that."

"I bet your boss called you at the marina, when Tiff and I were searching for the *Outlaw*."

Jason nodded. "I thought the marina was a secure hiding place, until you came along. So I moved the *Outlaw* into hiding on Hidden Island and painted out the name. I probably should have done that earlier, right after I firebombed the *Amor de Cosmos*."

"How'd you know there was an abandoned boathouse on the island?" I asked.

"Pepper told me."

"And where'd you keep your truck?"

"On different side streets in Oak Bay."

"You never got your money, eh? What a shame."

Jason ignored my sarcasm. "My boss kept saying, *Wait, wait, wait*. Well, I'm sick of waiting." He looked across the water. I could see the pilot boat approaching the beautifully illuminated *Romance of the Seas*.

"Tonight," Jason said, "we're boarding that ship. I'll waste my boss and take control of the painting. I'll be the one who sells it for big money."

Jason looked at me. There was evil in his eyes. "And when I don't need a hostage anymore, you'll die, too."

13

At low throttle, the *Outlaw* wallowed in the ocean swells. We watched the pilot boat slide alongside the cruise ship, then the pilot jumped onto the cruise ship through the open door in its side. Immediately the boat turned away and began its journey home to port.

Jason cranked up the throttle; with a throaty roar, our boat closed quickly on the cruise ship. "When we reach that door," Jason yelled, "you jump in first. I'll be right behind. If you try to escape, I'll start killing people."

The *Romance of the Seas* loomed over us, so huge. I could hear its engines, and the slap of waves against the luxury vessel's massive steel hull. As the big door came closer, I got ready to jump. I was so tense I could hardly breathe.

"Don't betray me," Jason warned, "or everyone dies."

Suddenly we were beside the open door, and I leapt across. Landing safely, I turned to see Jason jump. The empty *Outlaw* began drifting away and was quickly lost in the night.

Nearby were some crewmen, their backs to us. They were shouting advice and encouragement at a television screen, where two teams chased a soccer ball across a green field. Jason gestured at a nearby corridor. "Let's get moving, before they see us."

We hurried through the sleeping ship; Jason's gun was hidden inside his black jacket. I could hear the muffled vibration of the engines—a constant thrumming somewhere far below. "You saw Paris here earlier?" Jason abruptly asked.

I nodded.

"Where?"

"On the Royal Deck, in the Suite of Dreams."

"You think he's on board now?"

"Maybe," I replied. "He was talking that way."

"Take me to the suite."

Quite a few people wandered the ship at this late hour. In the Grand Atrium four seniors were enjoying a game of cards, while a couple waltzed dreamily on a corner dance floor. No one paid the slightest attention as I boarded a glass-enclosed elevator with Jason and pushed the button for the Royal Deck.

"Why do you want Paris?" I demanded. "Is he your boss?"

"Shut up."

After a quick journey to the heights of the vessel,

the elevator doors hissed open. I saw the deep purple carpeting, the wide corridor, and the creamy doors of the suites with elaborate names. One door stood slightly open, and I looked inside. Room service was delivering a late-night snack. It was going to the suite where I'd seen the metal tube being delivered.

The waiter walked quickly to the elevator. Watching him go, I said nothing and didn't cry for help. I was afraid I'd get the waiter shot, because Jason had sneaked his gun out of hiding.

We continued walking along the corridor in the direction of the Suite of Dreams. As we did, I struggled to deal with a new shock—I had recognized the person who received the room service delivery.

* * *

From behind, I heard a sound. I turned to look, so did Jason—gripped in his hand was the shiny revolver. Something was tossed from a suite onto the carpet, and landed with a soft *thump*. I saw the Laughing One, her village and its totems.

"Hey," Jason said. "That's the painting!"

Hurrying forward, he picked it up. "Yes, this is *Klee Wyck*. But how . . ."

At that moment, someone stepped swiftly from the suite. Someone in a floppy hat and sunglasses, someone in an expensive blouse and designer jeans. The metal tube was raised high.

It came down hard across Jason's hand.

With a cry of pain, he dropped the revolver. I leapt for it, but the other person was quicker than me. Seizing the gun from the floor, she levelled the scary weapon at Jason, who was rubbing away the pain in his hand.

"Don't move," the woman warned. Turning to me, she gestured at the painting. "Roll it up, Liz. Put it inside the tube."

As I rolled up the painting, tears were streaming down my face. I felt so betrayed, because I had been tricked by someone I trusted.

The woman removed the sunglasses, and I saw her large, dark eyes. Then she tossed away the hat. Auburn hair tumbled down her back. I was looking at Laura Singlehurst.

* * *

"Pick up the mailing tube," Laura ordered me.

"Laura, how could you? I respected you, and—"

"*No talking*."

Laura turned quickly to Jason. He stood beside the wall, still rubbing his hand. "Jason," she demanded, "what are you, crazy?"

"I do all your dirty work, boss, then you skip town with the painting."

"You'd have got your money, once I sold *Klee Wyck*."

"I doubt it," Jason scoffed. He stared daggers at Laura. "I was hoping I'd find you through Paris, but this was better. Why'd you come out of hiding?"

"Liz saw me. I figured she'd tell you, and I'd be trapped. I saw your gun and decided to get it. That's why I threw the painting into the corridor—to distract you."

"Are Paris and the Major on board now?" I asked.

"No. I saw them leave the ship before it departed from Victoria."

Jason took a step toward Laura, but her finger tightened on the trigger. He paused, looking apprehensive. "Take it easy, Laura. That thing is dangerous."

Laura pointed at the outside door. "We're going on deck. You two go first, I'll follow behind. If I need to, I'll use this gun."

"Laura," I said, "don't be foolish. Give yourself up, please."

"I already qualify for hard time in prison, Liz. That's not for me—I'll find a way to escape. Now pick up that tube, and let's get moving."

Outside on deck, the night was beautiful. Millions of stars were radiant over the sea, where I saw the lights of other vessels. From far below I heard waves rushing away from the hull.

"We're going to the bridge," Laura said. "Get moving."

I tried to think of a plan. Could I somehow use the metal tube against Laura? How would Jason react? Would Laura start shooting?

"Laura," I said, stalling for time, "why did you do it?"

"I needed money to start a new life. A new identity, a new country. No more maxed-out credit cards, no more unpleasant guys pounding on my door demanding I repay their loans. I was frightened, Liz, I was desperate. Stealing *Klee Wyck* was a great idea."

"You didn't earn plenty as a lawyer?"

"There's never enough money."

"When I first met you, Laura, you said someone had

called your cell phone, and a ransom was being demanded. I should have wondered how the criminal knew your cell number—I guess it was Jason who called."

"That's right."

"You set me up to recover the forged painting at Butchart Gardens?"

"Yes," Laura replied.

"Come to think of it, you almost gave yourself away. The note at Butchart Gardens was written in emerald ink. When I first met you, I noticed the ink in your pen was the colour of your green car." I shook my head, disappointed with myself. "I bet Fossilized Pete told you about taking Tiff and me to West Bay Marina. You must have called Jason and warned him to escape."

"That's right."

I looked closely at her. "Did you know Jason attacked me in the cemetery?"

Laura was shocked. "I had no idea." She turned to him. "You fool!"

Jason laughed angrily. "You're the fool, Laura. If you'd paid me, I'd be home in Seattle right now and you'd be sailing happily to Alaska with the Emily Carr masterpiece. Instead we're in bad shape."

"I agree *you're* in bad shape," Laura retorted. "But I'll get out of this—just watch me. I'm very resourceful."

"Laura," I said, "why'd you keep the original *Klee Wyck* in hiding at Thirteen Oaks, instead of somewhere else?"

"If the forgery was ever detected and a search started for the original, Thirteen Oaks was the perfect hiding place. Who'd ever look there?"

"You had the original—why didn't you skip town immediately?"

"The collector in Alaska made that a condition. He wanted the *Klee Wyck* replaced with a forgery, so there'd be no uproar about the theft. He told me to stay in Victoria, to see if anyone noticed the forgery. I decided to wait until after the wedding, then leave town."

"You're planning to start a new life in Alaska?"

Laura shook her head. "No, I'm heading for Hawaii. I love those glorious flowers down there. I'll get my money from that collector, then fly south pronto."

Central command for the *Romance of the Seas* was the bridge, the place where the officers and pilot safely guided the massive ship. A sign warned *No Passengers Allowed*, but it didn't stop us. The door was unlocked; Laura opened it and we entered the bridge, to the surprise of the people inside. An officer in a white uniform turned to us, saying, "What the . . ." Someone else shouted, "She's got a gun."

Stepping swiftly behind me, Laura pinned my neck with her arm. With her other hand, she pointed the revolver at my head. "No false moves," she warned, "or this girl dies."

The officer looked at Laura. "What do you want?" she asked in a calm voice.

"Contact the Coast Guard and order a medical evacuation. Tell them to send a helicopter immediately."

The officer picked up a radio microphone. "*Romance of the Seas* calling Canadian Forces, 19-Wing Comox. Come in, please. We are requesting evacuation of a heart attack victim."

"No fake messages," Laura warned her. "Don't get smart."

"Stay calm," the officer replied. "Think about surrendering that gun to me. It's the smart thing to do."

"Forget it," Laura snapped. "I'm not going to prison."

Laura released my neck, but held me close with a firm grip. She looked at the officer. "This ship has a prison cell?"

"A brig? Yes."

Laura pointed at Jason with the revolver. "Put this kid under arrest. Police in Victoria want him for numerous crimes."

"Including abduction," I said, "and sinking the *Amor de Cosmos*."

The officer gave an order, and Jason was quickly hustled away. He gave me a dirty look, but went silently. I breathed a sigh of relief, even though the situation remained volatile.

I looked at the pilot, who hadn't spoken since we entered the bridge. "Why did the pilot boat take you to the cruise ship?" I asked. "You could have walked on board."

"My wife is in hospital, so I was delayed. The ship sailed without me, knowing I could board from the pilot boat."

"Is your wife okay?"

"You bet," he replied. "We have a little girl, Mary." He smiled briefly.

Long minutes passed while we awaited the helicopter. Various screens and radars glowed inside the dimly lit bridge; through the big windows I saw the first traces of dawn's light, bringing the promise of a beautiful day. As pale colours slowly came to the eastern skies, the jagged outline of a mountain range appeared.

"Here they come," said the officer. Through binoculars, she studied the approaching helicopter, which was large. "They'll drop a stretcher down for the victim, then winch it back up."

"I'll be in the stretcher," Laura said, "with the gun and the *Klee Wyck*. When I reach the helicopter I'll take control. They can fly me to land, and I'll escape with the painting."

"Give up," I pleaded. "You'll never reach safety, Laura. Someone could get hurt on that helicopter—maybe you."

"No more chatter, Liz. Bring the metal tube with you, and keep quiet."

Laura looked around at the others. "All of you, listen up. I'm going outside with this girl and the officer. If you radio a warning to the helicopter, they will both die. Then I'll shoot myself—I'd rather be dead than in prison."

Outside, Laura turned to the officer. "Where will the stretcher be lowered?"

"Aft, at the tennis courts."

Hovering over the *Romance of the Seas*, the rescue helicopter made an enormous racket, its rotors pounding against the air. A door opened in the belly, then someone waved to the officer. A stretcher appeared and dropped swiftly down.

"It's not too late," the officer told Laura. "Give yourself up."

"Laura," I suddenly exclaimed. "The tube is empty—the painting is gone."

She turned to me, confused. "What?"

I held out the tube. "Look inside—the *Klee Wyck* is missing!"

As Laura leaned toward the mailing tube, I snapped it sideways, catching Laura's wrist a solid blow. The revolver flew up high; leaping forward, the officer grabbed the gun in midair. Quickly she turned and faced Laura with the revolver.

"It's all over now," she said quietly. "You're under arrest."

Laura burst into tears.

14

One year later, I attended Tiffany's wedding to Hart deMornay. She had requested a spiritual service, so Hart arranged for a ceremony at Victoria's Christ Church Cathedral, one of the largest churches in the nation.

Paris did not attend the ceremony. An audit of the deMornay trust had revealed crooked dealings by Paris, who had secretly drained a lot of money from the trust to finance his shameful ways. Paris left Victoria in disgrace, and now lived in Britain on a small remittance provided by his brother and sister.

Hart had quickly declared his devotion to Tiffany. She shared his feelings, but was determined to be certain of their love. Consequently they had spent much of the year hanging out and getting to know each other, making sure they would be equals in their relationship. They did all kinds of neat things—windsurfing, hiking the West Coast Trail, and even exploring the crystal-clear ocean depths at Powell River in matching scuba outfits.

As for me, I'd stayed in close touch with William. We'd exchanged e-mails and letters, and talked on the phone. At Christmas, William flew to Winnipeg for a wonderful reunion. When I arrived for Tiff and Hart's wedding, I was thrilled to see him waiting at the Victoria airport with pink roses for me.

Tiff's mother had come from Grand Cayman Island for the ceremony and was seated inside the cathedral in a place of honour close to the Major. The vaulted ceiling rose overhead, and the stained-glass windows glowed with the glory of love. The blues were so blue, the greens so green, the reds so pure and rich.

Now, at 18, I was the maid of honour. Kate Partridge had graciously allowed me the privilege. She was now Tiff's principal attendant, and stood with the other attendants to the left of the bride. To the right of the groom were the best man and the ushers. One was William, looking so handsome in a beautifully tailored tuxedo.

William caught me staring, and we exchanged a smile. Then I returned my focus to the service, which was moving and splendid. When Tiffany and Hart exchanged their first married kiss, everyone cheered and the bishop grinned. We all knew this marriage was made in heaven.

Flower girls scattered rose petals down the aisle for the newlyweds, and the cathedral bells pealed in celebration as we gathered outside in the sunshine. As I talked to William, a ladybug landed on my arm, a lucky sign of more happiness to come. There were hugs and kisses and photo opportunities, and waves from passing tourists, then the wedding party piled into white stretch limousines and we took off through Victoria, yelling from the open windows. It was such a relief that the wedding had gone perfectly!

The reception was held at the Crystal Garden, just behind the Empress Hotel. Long ago this had been a famous swimming pool; now it contained tropical vegetation and was home to flamingoes, lemurs, and even the Golden Lion Tamarin monkey (looking at its bright eyes, I was reminded of Emily Carr's Woo).

At the south end of the Crystal Garden was a hardwood dance floor and many large tables; here everyone gathered for delicious food followed by dancing. The Major had brought in two bands for the occasion. One was Victoria's own Big Band Trio, which played great rock, and the other treat was Gator Beat, with authentic Cajun music from deep in the American southlands. Everyone was into it, from kids to grandparents, dancing and singing. What a celebration.

I danced mostly with William. He'd given evidence against Jason, who was in prison. So, sadly, was Laura. William had been sentenced to community service for his misdeeds, and was conducting art classes for seniors.

"They're wonderful students," William said, as we danced together. He was so handsome. "Now I'm hoping to combine my art with teaching."

"William, there's something I've been wanting to ask. For a year, actually."

His eyebrows rose. "What's that?"

"Remember at your studio, you swept some photos into a desk drawer and locked it?"

"Sure."

"Well, I've been wondering . . . Well . . ."

"Go ahead, Liz. You can ask me."

"Were they pictures of some girl?"

William roared with laughter. "Not a chance. I took those Polaroids for reference, as I worked on the forgery of *Klee Wyck*."

"That's all they were?" I said, greatly relieved.

"You're the only girl for me, Liz."

What good news! Now I felt quite chatty. "It's so nice your mom's health is better," I commented brightly. William had sold a painting for a large amount of money and used it to finance getting his mother to Arizona.

"Yes," William said. "Things are going well for my mom."

Things were also good for Tiffany's dad, who was with Marjorie. She'd introduced him to high society in Austin, Texas, where they now lived. "I'm very happy," the Major told me later, as we waltzed together. "You know, I almost sacrificed Tiffany to my romantic imagination. I honestly thought she'd be happy married to Paris. All that stuff about gambling really shocked me. Liz, what a fool I was."

"Tiffany's certainly happy now," I tactfully replied.

"I just hope Paris learned something, and is happy in Britain." A whimsical smile crossed the Major's face. "I remember Paris as a boy—he was such a nice kid."

"I guess people can change," I said. "Tiff was smart enough to recognize that."

"You're a good friend to Tiffany, Liz. I apologize for my sarcasm about your hyperactive imagination. That was rude of me."

"No problem," I said lightly. "I've been called worse."

"What about you, Liz? Any wedding bells in the future? Can I hope to attend another wedding soon?"

"William and I are taking it easy on that one, Major Wright." Then my face split into a big smile. "But so far, so good!"

"Wonderful," the Major exclaimed. "You deserve nothing but the best."

Next I danced with the happy groom. "Guess what," Hart said. "Tiff and I have given the estate a new name—Two Oaks." He smiled. "When our first baby arrives, the estate will become Three Oaks."

"I like it. The old name never appealed to me, perhaps because of my slightly superstitious nature."

"We've recovered the portrait of my mother, and it's back on display at the mansion. Pepper decided to live on Hidden Island with Amanda so we built them a nice cottage. Tiff and I have also invested some money in Pepper's dream to have her own recording studio."

"That's wonderful," I said.

After the dance, we joined Tiffany. She was so happy. I hugged her, then Hart. "Why aren't you Lord deMornay? You're the right type—kinda regal, you know?"

"The title belongs to Paris as the oldest child, but I don't care." Hart brushed Tiff's forehead with a kiss. "What matters is that I found my Lady, and we'll always be together."

I wished Tiff and Hart great happiness (later, she threw me her bouquet of trumpet-shaped calla lilies) and then I joined Pepper at a mouth-watering display of desserts.

"I was so worried," she told me, "about facing criminal charges for helping Jason steal the painting. But instead I got community service. I've been helping street people."

Pepper's eyes travelled to a table where her little girl sat with Caleb, the best man. Amanda was laughing happily as Caleb performed a trick of magic. "Amanda's the light of my life," she said, smiling fondly at her daughter.

"How's the music business?"

"I've signed my first artist. We saw her at Beacon Hill Park, giving a concert for the trees."

"I remember. Her songs were so good."

"Liz, thanks for all the e-mails. You've been a pal."

We joined William at a table. He was talking to his teacher—the noted Victoria artist Robert Amos, who was a great friend of Hart deMornay. Robert, of course, hadn't known about William's actions, but had some interesting insights about the technical aspects of his forgery.

"Emily Carr painted on both canvas and paper," Robert explained. "William used acrylic paint, which dries immediately and is very flexible if a canvas is rolled up—but William was smart enough to make it look like oil. With scientific instruments, the forgery could have been detected, but to the people at Thirteen Oaks it looked exactly like the original."

"Two Oaks," I corrected him, laughing. "And hopefully by next summer it'll be Three Oaks."

One last surprise remained, the perfect ending to a perfect wedding. Glancing at his watch, William jumped up from the table. "Liz, we must hurry."

Together we rushed outside—the night was warm. People wandered along Douglas Street; some were window-shopping, while others gazed at a beautiful horse and carriage waiting outside the Crystal Garden. The driver wore a top hat and tuxedo.

"Please step inside our carriage," William said, smiling at me. "We're leaving for a mystery destination."

"Really? Wow."

What a luxury it was, riding through downtown Victoria in that splendid carriage. In my beautiful dress I felt like a character in a fairy tale, especially when we passed the Inner Harbour and I looked up at the towers of the Empress Hotel. Enjoying the slow *clip clop* of our horse's hooves, I sighed at the sight of the exquisite lights outlining the Legislative Buildings.

Passing Carr House, with its gingerbread decorations, I thought of Emily Carr as a young girl and wondered if she could have anticipated the many twists and turns of a life that would bring such fame. Her genius and determination had inspired William to become an artist, and I felt certain that great success also awaited him.

"Happy?" William asked.

"Mmm," I whispered, cuddling close. "We're living a dream."

Along Dallas Road we followed the cliffs, watching lights on the distant shoreline. In the sky was a quarter moon—such a romantic sight. The minutes passed quickly, and finally we arrived at Ross Bay Cemetery, where our carriage stopped.

As we stepped from the carriage, I looked at the cemetery, feeling confused but trusting William. Above us, the silhouettes of trees moved gently in a light wind. Holding hands, we walked into the cemetery and soon reached our destination.

"We're at Emily Carr's grave," I said.

William nodded. "This is a special place, Liz. That's why I wanted to visit here tonight. I'm praying that Emily Carr will bless us both."

I hugged William and kissed him. "William," I whispered, "I think she already has."

Websites to Visit

Tourism Victoria:	tourismvictoria.com
Maritime Museum:	mmbc.bc.ca
Art Gallery of Greater Victoria:	aggv.bc.ca
Craigdarroch Castle:	craigdarrochcastle.com
Butchart Gardens:	butchartgardens.com
Carr House:	emilycarr.com
Victoria A.M.:	victoriaam.com
Royal B.C. Museum:	rbcm1.rbcm.gov.bc.ca
Crystal Gardens:	bcpcc.com/crystal
Hospice Society:	victoriahospice.com
TerrifVic Jazz Party:	terrifvic.com
Robert Amos:	robertamos.com
Eric Wilson:	ericwilson.com

About the Author

Flo and Eric Wilson in Victoria

For many summers, Flo and Eric have enjoyed welcoming cruise ship passengers to Victoria, where they met and still live. Together they researched the attractions featured in *The Emily Carr Mystery*.

Eric's roots are deep in the city he describes in these pages. His mother was born in Victoria; along with her sisters, she grew up there in the days of Emily Carr.

If you visit *www.ericwilson.com* you can read the exciting opening chapters of all the Eric Wilson mysteries.

THE ICE DIAMOND QUEST

A Tom and Liz Austen Mystery

ERIC WILSON

The yacht, driven by its power, was closing in fast. Ahead, the sea roared against a low reef, throwing white water into the dark night.

Why is a mysterious yacht flashing a signal off the coast of Newfoundland on a cold November evening? Tom and Liz Austen, with their cousins, Sarah and Duncan Joy, follow a difficult trail toward the truth. As they search, someone called the Hawk and people known as the Renegades cause major problems, but the cousins press on. In the darkness of an abandoned mine and later on stormy seas, they face together the greatest dangers ever.

"I read *The Ice Diamond Quest* and now I'm hooked on books."

—*Tamara K., Lachine, Québec*

ESCAPE FROM BIG MUDDY

A Liz Austen Mystery

ERIC WILSON

The air was blasted by thundering engines as the gang raced past us, escaping the scene.

I turned to my aunt: "Holy Hannah! I can't believe what just happened!"

Former Death Machine biker Billy Bones grabs Liz Austen's arm and whispers: "The password . . . is . . . NOEL. Remember it!"

Remember it? How could she forget?? That one word launchs an unforgettable road trip across Saskatchewan aboard the *Mañana Banana* and plunges Liz and her Métis friend, Marie, into a deadly world of kidnapping, international smuggling, and biker gangs with murder on their minds. The question is: will the girls elude the bikers' clutches and escape the dangers of Big Muddy?

"This book rocks!"

—*Chelsea D., Black Creek, British Columbia*

THE CASE OF THE GOLDEN BOY

A Tom Austen Mystery

ERIC WILSON

Headlights shone in the distance: a police car, moving fast. It swerved to a stop by the curb, then Officer Larson leapt out and ran swiftly inside. What was going on?

An investigation into the kidnapping of his schoolmate leads young Tom Austen to the seedy Golden Boy Café and an unexpected encounter with a desperate criminal. After getting one step too close to the kidnappers, Tom is taken prisoner and needs all his wits to survive.

The adventures of Tom and Liz Austen are followed by fans of all ages across Canada and abroad in countries like Spain and Japan. Voted 1992 Author of the Year by the Canadian Booksellers Association "for introducing children to the different regions of Canada," Eric Wilson has shown many young people the delights of reading.

"It was fantastic, wonderful, breathtaking, stupendous, amazing, and very, very hard to put down. I liked it so much I skipped breakfast to finish it off."

—*Seth R., Massey, Ontario*